Ganymede
Abducted by the Gods
Book One of the Fantastic Immortals Series

By

Wendy Rathbone

Ganymede: Abducted by the Gods Copyright © 2017 by Wendy Rathbone and Eye Scry Publications

Cover design: Sadie Sins

A publication by:
Eye Scry Publications
www.eyescrypublications.com

ISBN # 978-1-942415-18-3
TITLE: Ganymede: Abducted by the Gods
Author: Wendy Rathbone

Address all inquiries to the author at:
wendy@eyescrypublications.com

Acknowledgments

I'd like to give a special thank you to **Sadie Sins** for this book's beautiful cover.

Also, thank you to **Christina E. Pilz** for a wonderful beta-read of this novel.

And last but not least, thank you **Della Van Hise** for help with formatting and uploading all my published books. I couldn't do this without you.

Ganymede...*who was the loveliest born of the race of mortals, and therefore the gods caught him away to themselves, to be Zeus' wine-pourer, for the sake of his beauty...*

--Homer, **The Iliad**

1. The Farmer-Prince

I am a mortal who has become immortal. I cannot remember every detail of my long and continuous life, but there are aspects and events that stand out, especially the period during and after I was taken forever from my home. I was kidnapped by a powerful god, and fell in love with another. It happened longer ago than the reach of Earth history. And because of the bent and curved nature of time, I know firsthand that years passing as they relate to Earth do not match when you are taken to the realms of the gods.

I remember this of my life before I was taken:

Dymos, my little brown and white dog.

The fields in summer, tender and sweet.

A dewdrop blue sky.

Our great farm-kingdom of Tros, seemingly endless when I was small.

I can still smell the lilacs by the castle door, and hear my sister, Cinth, calling for me out in the meadow, her voice tangled in the white and golden locks of the asphodel blooms. "Gan. Gan," she'd call, and race right by my hidden spot, her dark hair and white chiton trailing on the wind.

I remember even though I was a prince I learned farming. I was a proficient hunter as well. I learned the bow and the sword. But I loved books more, especially of the philosopher's stone variety (not that I believed in magic, mind you), those types of books that took the idea of philosophy and the stone's possible elixir of knowledge inward toward gnosis, where every sentence made you stop, ponder, think. Thus, my favorite thing to do was lie on my back in the spring and summer far a-field and lose myself in the endlessness that made up the sky. I could not stop thinking of my favorite deep wisdoms, and wondering what was beyond here and now.

Sometimes I would lie naked in the wild grasses, for there was no nudity taboo in Tros, until my sun-dazzled skin pinked to bronze and my hair fell about my shoulders in even paler shades of gold.

I was the lightest child of all the family. None of them burned from mere daylight; they were all brunet and olive-toned. My coloring was rare. Even my eyes were a lighter version of theirs, copper instead of brown, green-flecked instead of shadowed.

I remember feeling odd a lot of the time, not beautiful enough, and despite being the son of a wealthy farmer-king, I believed I would not amount to much. I had no idea there were those unknown to me who thought my beauty rivaled even that of the gods.

The King of Tros, my father, knew what I was worth. An ambitious man, King Laomedon had a mind more for wealth and gain than loyalty or love.

I was newly eighteen the day my father sold me to the king of the gods. My price? A herd of storm-footed horses. Great beasts, to be sure. Unearthly. Puffing blue mist from their wide, round nostrils. Stomping the ground with silver hooves. Each one worth ten times what my father already owned.

I will say this. Secretly, I did not believe in gods, sacrifice, or manipulation from on high. I knew no one who had ever met a god. All my life I saw only hard-working people, their joys and humor, their diseases, their griefs. The natural way, I observed, was that people lived and died, and too often they suffered. If gods existed, why would they allow pain? Why death?

So it came as a great surprise to me to discover I was wrong.

2. A Bath and Some Clothes

I had no idea that my father was in negotiations over me. Or that he'd ever intended to sell me.

On my eighteenth naming day, I rose naked from the fields during an afternoon of lazy sun bathing, having avoided my little sister for the better part of the day. 18 was a pinnacle age to reach, and I had wanted time alone. I did not want to play. Evening approached and the first green star winked on the orange horizon. The asphodels bloomed sweet and yearning about me. Faraway, I thought I heard the sonorous note of a swan. The swan is my birth bird, both an air and water sign. It symbolizes beauty and transformation. Fitting to hear one on my naming day.

I headed for the baths. Later, I would don my best ribbon-trimmed chiton and summer cloak. I looked forward to the feast on my behalf where I would receive gifts, get drunk on Athiri wine, maybe flirt with a boy or two, or a girl if her smile caught my eye.

The royal baths for our family and friends were communal, filled with mineral water from surrounding springs, and said to soothe not only the body, but to heal it. The outbuilding that contained the baths was built from terra cotta bricks, but inside were marble floors and white columns surrounding five blue pools which were separated by fountains, benches and drying stations. The middle pool was the biggest and the coldest. It was where I headed on this hot mid-summer day. I had no clothes, so I did not need servants. Two stood ready to aid, both male, and I waved them off.

It was poor manners to sully the water with dirt, so I first rubbed my body with olive oil. I took a metal, curved tool and scraped the dirt and oil from my skin. I did this myself. I did not enjoy the hands of servants unless it was necessary.

My skin was hot. As I cleaned myself, my sunburn stung. But it wasn't too bad. My shoulders had gotten the worst.

When I was clean and glistening, I walked into the pool.

The cool water lapped me, fizzing a little from the clay salts. I floated toward the center and rinsed, then sat soaking on a waist-high underwater ledge, letting the faint lavender scent of the pool relax me and soothe my flaming skin.

I looked up toward the far wall where a mosaic of nymphs bathing in a tree-shaded glade took up most of the space. On the next wall a centaur watched over the room. I did not believe in such creatures, but they were sweet fantasies. I loved to read stories about their trials, their wars, their loves.

The wall sconces were all lit. Great braziers kept the place warm in winter, but were empty now. Lanterns flickered all around the pools. Despite the white marble floors, and the openness of the walls, shadows wavered, encroached. Everything echoed here, the water kissing the pool edge, the fountains with their sculptured lion mouths gently trickling water into their basins, the two men talking, side by side, in the warming pool off to my left. I recognized them as my father's aides, and ignored them as they did me.

When I was almost ready to leave, I dunked and scrubbed at my long hair. It trailed against my chest and shoulders in honeyed hanks. I smoothed all of it away from my face, intending to clip it back later when I dressed.

As I exited the pool, a male servant with short, dark bangs handed me a linen towel.

"Do you require assistance, Prince?"

"No."

I took the towel and headed toward the indoor hall that connected directly to the castle, drying myself along the way, then draping the cloth about my hips.

I saw guards and servants along the way to my rooms, but I did not see my sister, or any of my three brothers.

My favorite servant, Aeson, greeted me as I entered my chamber. "You are just in time," he said. Candlelight shimmered over his dark, shoulder-length hair. "I thought you might be late."

Yellow flames of candles swayed on tables and my desk, and on the shelf above my curtained bed. The lanterns were all lit. My balcony doors stood open, and the last dim light of the day cast its topaz longing about the room.

"Am I ever late?"

Aeson laughed. He was a friend from childhood and he took care of me. He knew me well. In truth, I was more often late than early to any function, including ones held on my behalf.

He had my chiton and green cloak and leather sandals waiting. I was dressed within minutes, including jewelry and belt, with time enough leftover for him to comb my wet hair, pull it back and twist it into an elaborate braid. He was careful in his ministrations, which was why I kept him on. He knew I was not one for casual touch. I did not like hugging, petting, or the openness to sex my father and brothers enjoyed. Maybe it was because I was the youngest. Maybe it was my coloring that gave me pause and made me insecure, prudish.

I put up with touches from my mother out of politeness.

The only person I let hug me or touch me at will was my little sister, who was sweet as spring.

I enjoyed flirting with other courtiers my age, but then I was done. I never followed through. I never took a boy or girl, not once, to my bed.

No one spoke of this. No one dared. We all pretended everything about me was normal.

When Aeson was finished with my hair, he stood back and assessed me with a smile and a wink. "You are breath-taking like no other before you."

He always said things like that. I always accused him of flattering me for a wage raise.

"Well," I answered, brushing my hand over the ruby bracelet on my wrist. "It'll do."

"May your naming night contain all you wish for."

"We're both eighteen now. Do you ever think much further into the future?" We'd talked of subjects like these before, but not in depth. He was my companion more in childhood tutoring, but rarely did I divulge to him my deepest, more personal thoughts. Beyond that he kept my rooms clean.

"I would like a wife and children, I think, some day."

"I'm sure you'll have them," I said.

"And you?"

"No. I don't plan ahead. And I'm far far back in succession to be king. I think I'm pretty lucky. I have everything I need, and I can do as I wish. Why should I worry about marriage or anything like the future?" But in truth, my name day had me thinking about just those subjects while lying in the field all afternoon.

"You're young and you have time. Some day you will discover what you want and take it," Aeson said.

"I suppose you're right."

I turned away, staring out the balcony doors to the last strip of magenta sky on the distant horizon. I could smell fresh bread cooking from the kitchens, and beeswax, and the lavender that still clung to my skin. In this single moment, everything seemed perfect.

3. Naming Day Feast

Before I reached the banquet hall, I could hear the chatter of the gathered guests, the clinking of the chalices, the shuffling of leather on marble as people moved about. When I came to the entrance, brightness filtered throughout the room from sconces, oil lamps, and elaborate candelabra. The room had a high ceiling painted eggshell-blue, and lining the white walls were marble statues of kings and queens, all made into gods in naked repose.

Aeson followed me into the hall. I had invited him to stand at my side for the night. He would serve me, but he would also partake of all the delicacies of the feast itself.

Cinth ran straight to me as if she'd been waiting all day, a princess of twelve with long black braids, my girl. My little mutt, Dymos, lolled in her arms, his tail madly wagging.

"Happy Naming Day," she said, shifting the dog and hugging me one-armed. "I want you to have my gift first!" From a pocket inside her long, white dress she brought out a tiny book sewn together with gilt thread. On it was painted one word. **Poems.** "I copied the ones that are your favorites and drew pictures beside them," she said, handing it to me. "I made my own poem to you at the end."

As much as I loved staring at the sky, I loved to read more.

I took the little book from her and leaned down, kissing the top of her head. "I love it. I don't care what else I receive tonight. This one will be my favorite."

Her smile grew; her brown eyes glowed. I had meant my words as truth. I already knew I would cherish this book for as long as I lived.

Suddenly I was surrounded by admirers and well-wishers, and Cinth and Dymos became lost in the crowd.

Banquet tables were set up in long rows to seat all my father's guests. The high table at the front of the room was where my mother and father would sit, with me as the guest of honor at my father's side, and my eldest brother Mikkos to my mother's left.

I saw a table by a statue of Dionysus covered with colorful, cloth-wrapped parcels. But I didn't care about them. I had Cinth's book. I had the feast for this evening. And I was living a life where no one had any expectations of me. I was a bit spoiled, and I liked it.

Someone handed me a chalice of wine and I realized as I took a deep drink that my whole life was laid out before me, unhindered, and I could make of it anything I pleased. My veins heated at the thought of such freedom. My heart thrummed.

My father approached. He wore a leather skirt that showed off his dark, muscular legs. His leather breast-plate, perfectly fitted, gleamed over his white shirt, topped by a heavy, black cape. His sandals fastened all the way to his knees. The evening was warm but he did not look at all uncomfortable.

"Ganymede," he said, embracing me as I stiffened under the touch. My mother, at his side, pressed a warm kiss to my cheek which I tolerated better. Almost too quickly, my father led me to the high table as if he wanted to get on with the night.

The guests took note of his ascension to the royal seats and all found their places.

He made a quick speech, ending with the usual, expected statement of pride. "My youngest son is a man today. I am proud of him. Later, I have another announcement to make that will make my family very happy. But for now, we feast!"

The crowd applauded approval.

The food could not have been better. Roasted meats and fowl dripping in their own juices, fresh breads soaked in olive oil, figs, grapes, oranges and more. Biscuits, iced cakes and puddings came later. The wine never ran out.

My brothers each approached bearing gifts. Mikkos with his sharply arched brows and high forehead, Palaemon who was lean and tall and could run faster than an approaching storm, and Thon, closest to my age who, at twenty-one, already held a wrestling championship in two districts. All were married but Palaemon, who preferred the company of men and had a beautiful lover named Zeno living in his rooms. But we all knew my father would force a marriage upon him before he turned 30, just as he would with me, if Palaemon and I did not take matters into our own hands and find suitable mates on our own.

I had had other siblings at one time. Two more brothers and a sister. None of them survived past infancy. Cinth was born when I was six. After that, Calli, my mother the queen, bore no more.

The dinner lasted a long time with many courses. It was a delirium of flavors, scents, and merriment. Performers came and went, putting on plays and lyrical concerts. The wine was less watered than usual and intoxication came on fast; the noise level rose.

When I could not eat another bite, I got up to talk with friends. I received many gifts: jeweled daggers and broaches and arm bands, fine cloth, brocade pillows, and offers of pleasure I could not count. Partiers mingled, socialized, or walked the fragrant gardens outside the hall, the air redolent with orchids and jasmine. The day had finally cooled.

Finally, my father ordered silence and rose from his high table. The guests, most of them the wealthiest of the upper class, gathered to listen.

Sconce-light caught the filaments of gray in my father's dark hair, making him look glamorous and ensorcelled. He began to speak.

"Tonight we honor my youngest son, Ganymede, on his eighteenth year. His intelligence and poise have never disappointed me or his mother. He honors us with his presence in our lives."

I'd heard Laomedon speak this way, but never of me. He showed his approval in smiles and nods, not public or private words. My skin heated from the wine, and from pride.

"To further honor my son, I would also like to announce I have made a deal with a far-off kingdom to which he will be ambassador. He will travel there, and his travels will bring us bounty and knowledge and wealth. Gan is my perfect choice for this honor and duty. He is intelligent, reasonable and well-liked by everyone."

For a moment I heard nothing, the hush of the great hall like a deep breath held. It was as if I was underwater and surrounded by nothing but blue-tinged liquid. I saw my father's lips still moving, but heard nothing more. A ringing began in the center of my head, vibrating in my ears.

Far-off kingdom. Travel. Ambassador. My mind turned the words over and over. My chest shuddered. Was I to leave my sister, my brothers, my parents, Tros, all that I had ever known? I could make no sense of any of this.

The people of Tros were all staring at me now, their eyes wondering, their bodies gleaming, precious jewelry glimmering. All privileged. All safe. Reveling in celebration. Including me. I had been one of them. The guest of honor. Until this very moment.

Now I would be leaving it all. Stepping into the unknown.

A soft hand slipped into mine, clammy, trembling. I knew by the touch it was Cinth. She squeezed tight. Then I heard her whisper, "Gan, Gan, is it true?"

I turned away, but her hand would not let me go. Dymos leaned against my shin.

My father had made this decision and never told me. My father was sending me away! I could not believe it.

I did not hear the rest of his speech. When sound returned, people were talking again. Cutlery rang against porcelain. Lyres strummed. Voices sang. Wine ran hand in hand with laughter. My brothers smiled and raised their cups to me.

My father beamed. An honor, he had said. But it felt more like punishment.

I escaped the hall as deftly as I could, head still reeling. Cinth followed with my dog. We entered a corridor that led to a great staircase. Here the air felt cooler and I took my first deep breath in what felt like hours. Cinth had her hand on my cloak and was saying earnestly, "Gan, why didn't you tell me?"

"I didn't know. I didn't know he was sending me away until just now."

"But why?"

I pulled away from her. "I don't know!"

Dymos stood panting, his pink tongue lolling. I would be leaving both of them, all of them, my whole family, friends and servants, and the only country I'd ever known. Why?

I didn't want this. Surely my father would hear my wishes, see reason, and send someone else. Just that one thought calmed me. I put my hand on Cinth's head, petting. "It's a mistake, that's all. I'll fix it. You'll see."

She smiled up at me, the adoration in her eyes something I had never taken for granted.

4. The Accord

From the time we were small children, my brothers, sister and I were entertained with stories of heroes and adventure and love. Exotic locales and fairytale kingdoms were peopled by men and women who were favored by the gods. Or if not favored, met with terrible fates and dark endings. Enchanted kings and shape-shifting witches. Mermaids and giants. Satyrs and nymphs.

One such story told of an enchanted bear who stole little girls and boys and kept them in an iron barred room with only pita bread to eat once a day. If he got very hungry, he might eat one or two of the children. If he became lonely, he would pick the more docile ones and make them his pets and train them to wait on him all day long and do whatever he said.

We were young, so the details about the misery and torture of victims was vague, and the fables always had happy endings. In the one about the bear, the children eventually revolted and stabbed the bear to death with dull knives and spoons. Just before he died, the bear turned into a beautiful young man who admitted he'd been cursed and thanked the children for putting him out of his misery. They cut off his head and put it on a pole and hiked back to town with it to show everyone. The children then made their way to their homes where they were received with love and healing support, and all proclaimed as heroes.

That story gave me nightmares. My brothers laughed. But for a long time I dreamed of a bear's head, battered and bloodied, showing his fangs as he spoke to me though I could never remember what he said. Eventually, I grew out of the bad dreams. I learned what metaphor was. I realized bears couldn't really speak, and if they killed you it only meant you were not a very good hunter.

I left my sister by the bottom of the castle stairs, and escaped unseen into my mother's private garden. My entire body had broken out in a sweat. The linen of my chiton clung to my back underneath my lightweight cloak. I did not feel at all well.

I needed to speak to my father, but not like this. I had to get myself under control.

The cool night air cleared my head and I kept taking deep breaths. Autumn was still far enough off that everything was luscious, green. I smelled wild pomegranate and laurel. The garden was shaded by olive and chestnut trees. White orchids bloomed on long stalks at the bases of their trunks. Water lapped the edges of a sprinkling fountain, silver in the moonlight. I stopped by that fountain and dipped my hand in, bringing the fresh dampness to my forehead. I wet my cheeks with my palms over and over again, trying to cool off.

Before now, I had never considered leaving my home. My family, my friends, the palace servants—they were my world. I might have spent a lot of time staring at the endless skies of Tros, but I always remained grounded when I did so in the fields of the lands of my birth. Now, just when I thought I had everything, it all had been taken away.

I was eighteen now, no longer a child. I kept reminding myself I wasn't being kidnapped by a bear, only instructed to make a voyage to a new place. Many would have been excited, seen the task as a wonderful challenge. A gift. But not me. Just the thought of leaving made a sort of hot panic rise in me. Maybe it was because I lacked the capacity for challenge. Or feared being not valued by my cool-hearted father, thrown away on a whim. Or maybe it was because I was truly afraid of the things I'd read and thought about, things that dwelt beyond the lands and skies I could see with my own eyes. My travels were limited to the stories I read. I felt secure among the parchments, and in my imaginings. Comfortable. I did not want to leave such comforts.

All I could think was that I needed to convince my father to send someone in my place. Surely Laomedon would see reason, understand my wish to remain in Tros. I had no need to panic. Yet.

But my heart would not rest in my chest. A strange, sharp pain struck me every time I took a breath. A stinging heat collected behind my eyes.

I don't know how long I stood by the fountain trying to orient myself, fight my fears and convince myself to turn around and go back to the party. I needed to confront my father.

All of this was so sudden and I had so many questions. He was a hard man, but what could have made him want to throw me away like this? With no warning?

Too much had gone unspoken. I had to speak to him.

After awhile, my body stopped shaking. The sweetness and the calm of the garden had helped.

I turned, looking up through tall tree branches that silhouetted the ink of the sky. Stars poked their light through a faraway barrier I could not conceive of. How far away was I expected to go? And could I make my father change his mind?

I headed through archways of vines and ivy to the garden door and into the atrium beyond. I walked a long corridor full of breathing shadows and lanterns of red flame. The oil kept burning but darkness crept into me anyway.

As I made my way into a more well-lit corridor, I began to hear the sounds of merriment again. I entered the great hall where people still laughed and drank, where musicians performed, where dancers wove gracefully about the room. I ignored it all, searching for my father in the crowd.

He was nowhere.

As I scanned the high table where we'd eaten, and every corner of the hall, Mikkos and Thon came up on either side of me, patting my back, drunk and grinning, both talking at once. "Where is Father sending you?" "Did you know about this all along?" "Why is he sending you?" "Have you displeased him?" Mikkos hair was wild and dark about his shoulders, perfectly straight. Thon had shorter hair that curled at the edges when the air was damp. He had a habit of tossing his head back as he spoke, more so when he was drunk, as if that gesture made his words more important than anyone else's.

"Have you seen him?" I asked, ignoring their questions.

"He left some time ago with his guards and several servants," Mikkos said.

"I need to see him."

"You won't see him tonight," Mikkos replied.

Thon added, "He is never to be disturbed after retiring for the night, you know that."

"Where's Mother?"

"You look worried," Thon said. "You didn't know, did you?"

"I have to speak with them, both of them. Tonight."

"You're in shock," Mikkos said. "Come with us."

My brothers hauled me over to the wine cask. I tried to pull away. "No. No more wine tonight. I've already been sick."

"You're a man now," Thon said. "Men don't get sick on wine."

Palaemon approached from the crowd. "Gan. I've been looking everywhere for you."

"He was sick, so he says," Thon offered.

18

Mikkos winced. "He didn't know about Father's announcement."

Palaemon clasped my shoulder despite knowing I didn't like to be touched. "I know. And I see on your face you're not happy. But Father's in the throne room and he wants to see you. Now."

"Now?"

"Come on." Palaemon put his arm around me and drew me forward. He seemed calmer than my other brothers, cooler, sober, and I went with him willingly, though I was still tense. I didn't try to pull away. He was only being supportive in the way he knew how. And right now I needed that. Mikkos and Thon hung back to make sure their chalices were wine-filled to the brim. They did not follow us.

Palaemon was taller than I, and pulled me along with his arm around my shoulders, the side of my head brushing his chin. His black hair hung shoulder-length and soft, his bangs long and half-covering his eyes. Normally I would not put up with his touch for so long, but I was so displaced by my father's announcement that the weight of his arm grounded me.

The throne room was in the west wing, toward the main double-doors at the front of the palace, and white statues lined the outside of the entrance, naked and tall, some gazing off into unfathomable distances, others seated and reading, but all bearing a cold, hard pride of immortality in frozen splendor. Our footsteps echoed on the marble floor.

We stopped at the threshold where two guards eyed us with alert stances, their spears blocking the way. We gazed back, Palaemon relaxed and somewhat brazen, me shy and unsure. "We're here to see the king at his command."

"He asked for Prince Ganymede only," one guard said, his gold helm gleaming under the oil-lights.

"Do you want me to come in with you?" Pal asked me, his arm on my shoulders lifting away.

"Yes." I said it quickly, without thought. I was still shaking, half of me left behind in the warm gardens under the trees and the velvet sky. I had such a horrible feeling of wrongness. I did not want to be here at my father's bidding. I had wanted to command an audience with him at a time of my own choosing.

Pal kissed me affectionately on the side of the head, a gesture he'd done only when we were very small but never in our teen years. Instead of stepping away and scowling as I normally would have, I moved closer to him. "I'm here," he whispered. Then he looked up at the guard who had spoken. "You heard him. I'm his advocate. We're inseparable."

The muscles around the guard's eyes tightened. The other guard glanced at him. They seemed to commune in some silent language of guard-gazing before the first finally grunted and moved to open the gold, ornate doors.

Pal and I had always been close. In fact I was close with all three of my brothers. We did not tattle on each other if things went wrong. We took the blame for things that weren't our fault. In essence, we had a great bond. I think the chilly demeanor of our father left us no choice. All of us were close, though Cinth was my favorite.

Once when Pal had been reprimanded to his rooms for a week for avoiding his tutors and not completing his lessons, we all took turns sneaking him treats. For hours I would sit at his door and play knucklebones and cards with him; we slipped each card played under the door, back and forth. Cinth, who'd been about four at the time, had asked, "Is Pal stuck? Is that why he can't get out?" I'd replied, "Yes, my love, but we're working on the problem."

Another time my father had been so angry at Mikkos for sneaking out at night and staying away until dawn that he had him whipped until the skin of his back opened. Surgeons had to treat him, and we all took turns by his side in shifts, never leaving him alone as he healed. It took two days before he would even speak to us, and two months before he spoke to our father again. Laomedon did not seem to notice.

Now Pal steered me into the open throne room. Its ceiling went up to the third story level, and was curved, part metal, part pale marble reflecting the sconce-lights. The king's throne sat upon a dais. Two sets of shallow stairs led up to it from the left and right. It was made of marble, gold-cushioned and topped with emeralds at its high back. My mother's throne was smaller, with rubies instead of emeralds, and more cushions to mold her smaller frame. The size of it always made me think that somehow she'd been cheated. When I was very small, I did not understand why she didn't have the biggest throne because after all she was my mother and mothers were beautiful, sacred, everything. That is what it is like when you are little and young and fathers are absent or cold.

Tonight my mother was not there. Laomedon sat alone in the huge, echoing chamber. I spotted six guards at the edges of the room, half-hidden by pillars. Two more were at attention to the left of the throne.

Standing between the thrones was a white-bearded old man with thinning hair that fluffed out from his head. He wore nothing but a long white robe. He had a crooked stick of hazel for a staff, unvarnished. But the strangest thing about him was the stunning raven on his shoulder. I had never known a raven to be a pet. This one sat very still as if it were not even alive, and its yellow eye—yes, yellow, not black—stared, as if right through me.

My father shifted in his seat, his face dark in the old man's shadow, his red cloak askew on his shoulders. He looked still young at fifty, his strong leg muscles bulging around his tightly laced, knee-length sandals, his arms crossed and the upper gold bands showcasing the muscle there as well. He could have been an older brother to all of us. The gray in his hair had barely yet begun.

"Palaemon," he said. "You may go."

Pal replied casually, as if unafraid, "Gan asked me to be here." In truth, we were all afraid of Laomedon.

I stared at the floor, waiting.

All my father said was, "I will not ask again."

"It might be good for him to see." The old man spoke. His voice filled the chamber in a redolent baritone and I did not understand how such a diminutive figure could have such power in speaking. "Palaemon is your other unmarried son?"

Laomedon leaned forward. "The deal was for Gan only."

"But if they both intrigue me?"

My father's eyes widened as I looked up. For the first time in my life, I saw fear in the king.

Pal's hand had dropped from my shoulder, but now he reached out and tightly gripped my wrist. He could smell it in the air, too. The wrongness. A wash of alien scent, something unknown and new and strange made the hairs stand up on my neck and arms. Something predatory.

I swallowed but my throat remained dry. "Father." My voice sounded like a strange croak. "I didn't know I was interrupting your meeting with this stranger. I wanted to speak with you about your announcement at my feast. Then Pal and I will leave you to your other guest."

The old man turned to look at me and my breath stopped. His eyes were blue like reflected light on a pond. I'd never seen such eyes. And they were bright as if there was a heat in them that was trying to break free and burn us all.

My father ignored my statement. He said to the old man, "I don't want them to know. Pal cannot know."

The old man kept staring at me. I clamped my teeth to keep from showing my nerves.

Under his breath, Pal said, "Gan, we need to go. I've seen something like this—"

"You cannot leave." The voice of the old man wove about the room. "The doors are all locked."

"Pal, what is it?"

"Silence!" The old man turned back to my father. "Your son Palaemon has seen me before. It's too late. He almost recognizes me. I can take away his memory if you'd like."

Pal began to back away, me in tow. "No," Pal said.

I turned back, sensing immediate danger. "Don't hurt my brother!" I said loudly.

"Ah, the youngest is bold, too. I like that. It heightens his beauty along with his sweetness and bashful avoidance of touch."

"What? Father—"

The old man interrupted me with his hand held up. "He has no say in this matter anymore. You will address me."

Pal had backed away, but remained close behind me, not quite touching now, his breathing fast.

"Who are you? Address you about what?" Bashful? I was becoming angry. My fear only fueled it.

From behind me, Pal said, "Gan, don't speak to him." I'd never heard his voice tremble so before.

"You have no say in this matter, either, Palaemon." The old man moved from between the thrones and approached the left staircase.

I felt Pal's hand touch the small of my back. Then it was gone. At first I thought I was dizzy, still drunk from the celebration. It was as if all the air left the room, all sound. Something smelled like burnt leaves.

My father looked like a dim painting. I couldn't hear Pal's breathing anymore.

It seemed as if I'd blacked out for suddenly the old man stood an arm's length away from me, his fiery blue eyes so vivid they blinded me for a moment. When I blinked, I saw the raven on his shoulder, unmoving, that yellow eye watching me.

Without warning, the man's staff came up under my cloak and yanked. It flew off my body and landed somewhere I could not see. I tried to lift my arms to defend myself, but they felt heavy, weighted, as if my body were encased in thick liquid.

My father watched from far away.

Do something! I tried to speak the words but my mouth would not cooperate. I tried to look for Pal but could no longer hear or see him.

The old man spoke again. "You will travel far and well, Ganymede. The sedation will make it easier."

Again the staff came up and I noticed the top was carved into a sharp blade. It cut through the cloth of my chiton at my shoulders, until it fell around my waist, held up now only by my leather belt. The gilt edges of the cloth glittered.

Despite the fact that clothing in Tros was optional, especially in high summer, I'd never felt more exposed.

The man smiled and his visage looked suddenly young, the beard fading, the hair darkening. His robe disintegrated as if it had been merely an image, a ghost upon his body. He stood naked, dark-eyed and dark-haired now, but for bracelets, rings and a small gold circlet spiking at the crown of his head.

His beauty could not be questioned. He tilted his head. His muscles moved under his skin in smooth waves as he reached up. "I collect things of rare beauty. You will come live with me now."

My question must've shown on my face. *How? Why me?*

"I made the deal with your father. A price he could not refuse. It's all set." As if from thin air, his free hand held a scroll. "Signed and copied. The deal is done. He called it our accord. You belong to me now."

My mind spun. I saw myself drinking too much at the party. Going to the garden. Splashing cool water from the fountain on my hot face. This had to be a dream. I had to have passed out, drunk. Surely, I was lying by the waving fronds of orchids beneath my favorite olive tree. I would wake soon from this nightmare.

I was a prince. My father would never sell me. Not me.

The image of the beautiful man before me began to fade. Yes. This was a dream. None of it could be real. Still, his voice echoed off the hard, cold walls. "He negotiated well. A herd of the finest horses fit only for the gods. Ten large cauldrons of gold." He smiled and his teeth were very white. "I think I got the better part of the deal." I could barely see him anymore. "Safe passage," he said, waving.

The raven moved then. I hadn't noticed the bird remained solid even as the man faded. It shook itself as if from its own dark dreamings, and unfurled pitch wings. It fluttered up into the air and the darkness of its body grew until it blocked my vision and all I saw was night without stars.

24

I had no idea yet that this raven being would become a major part of my life. All I could feel was fear and shock as I tried to cry out but had no voice.

The now giant raven's vast wings covered me. I felt a soft clasp, a satiny encasing all over my body. I wanted to scream. To fight. To cough against that softness as it seemed to invade even my mouth.

The last thing I heard before pure blackness settled over me was my brother Pal. He was yelling my name. "Gan! Gan!" But he sounded so far away.

5. Taken

My father called it an *accord* but actually he sold me so he could be the wealthiest king ever to rule over Tros. That is what I told myself. That is what I believed for a long, long time.

The story that had frightened me as a child was coming true, but it wasn't a bear who took me away. It was a god.

I have spoken of the raven. Myth says it was an eagle who took me up into the sky, but this is my myth and I was there. It was a raven. A glorious, alien raven.

He wrapped me tight in black-feathered limbs that extended separately from his wings. Darkness surrounded me, a tight embrace. I tried to scream but no sound came from me. My body shuddered, gasping for air. My eyes were wide open, trying to see, but failing.

The giant bird moved sideways. Pressed to him, I heard only a muffled hum, a life-pulse. I never heard doors open or guards yell. I did not know how we got out of the palace throne room, or if anyone but my father and brother ever saw us at all, but soon afterward my body jerked as if we were moving up, and I became instantly dizzy.

To say that I was scared would be an understatement. Even caught up in this strong grip, I was instinctively afraid of falling. I clung to soft feathers and down with my fists. He smelled of fresh grass, cool wind and again I had the thought that I'd actually passed out in my mother's garden and this was all part of some intoxicated dream.

I felt a fluttering in my head and my dizziness increased.

Turn your face.

Soft, low, the voice spoke in my mind. It resonated a gentleness, completely opposite from the voice of the stranger that had commanded my father in the throne room.

Turn your face.

I tried to move and found I could stretch my neck and drag my cheek over the soft feathers until my mouth found air, the wind whipping past, its dark chill upon my lips.

Take slow, deep breaths.

I gasped. Not slow. Fast. Panicking.

A mistake. Breathe slow.

But though the voice remained calm and mesmerizing, I could not obey.

Relax now. You will feel like you are dying, but you are not. You will not breathe again for some time.

The limbs tightened about me and my head was again pressed hard into black feathers which tangled into my mouth until I thought I would choke. Adrenalin rushed into me, stinging its way through my veins. Tears squeezed from between my closed eyelids.

Rest easy, sweet one. You are not dying. I would never allow that. I promise I will protect you always.

Though the voice was gentle, low and lulling, I could not believe him. *Sweet one.* Why would he call me that? My body struggled. Shook. More tears stung behind my eyes.

Sleep now, precious boy.

Instead of sleeping, I fainted.

*

I had a long dream of soaring. Floating. An abyss all around me.

I heard voices, some speaking to me, some randomly floating in the void.

"Your bird is the swan."

"His hair is flaxen fairy-gold."

"Eyes up. Chest out."

"Your lips are my wine."

One voice sounded like my brother Thon. "There are lions like statues in the hills."

I heard Dymos barking, my sister crying. I tried to yell but my voice was swept away as if by a giant shadowed tide of nothing.

The voices faded as soon as the waves of sound washed over me, echoing to tremulous whispers.

A deep voice boomed. "Travel by raven is flawless."

I felt my body tense, go limp, tense again. Over and over my muscles and sinew and flesh fought what was happening to me. My mind was open in a perpetual scream.

I fell in and out of consciousness. Every time I seemed to wake I found myself in the same position, clutching soft feathers, pressed tight to a silken chest. The arms around me felt human enough, but I knew it was a bird that held me, a strange raven who had grown to the size of a large man. Sometimes I felt no motion from him. Other times his body jerked up and down, side to side.

A voice said, "Make the jump."

Another, "He has folded space until it is the most delicate, budding rose."

Still another, "It's all in the math."

Then I heard *him* again in my mind. *Sun-like human, are you there?*

I could not utter even a groan.

Deep-eyed you are, with river nymphs in your veins. On your mother's side. Your mother's mother. This makes your blood smell of honey. It is not your fault. He takes what he wants. He collects the beautiful. Makes them his. But I will protect you. I swear it.

I did not understand the words at all. Did he mean my grandmother had been some sorceress? Many of my people believed in such things, but I never had. His descriptions continued, both confusing and soothing.

One time I woke and he was almost humming. I rode that song for a long time before I finally made out actual words. *Stop crying. Stop crying.*

After that, my plunge into blackness went deep. I lost myself in slow hours, streaming eons, dark ages.

When I woke again the dizziness began to fade.

There now. Shhh. The voice of comfort wove about my stuttering heart. *Turn your head. You can see now. Look. Just look.*

I was able to move again. My whole body arched. My head turned. The tight arms loosened. I could wiggle my legs. I still clutched hard at the breast feathers, but now I could see their iridescence—blue, green, purple—and feel the warm air against my bare back, my fluttering legs.

Between flaps of the raven's huge, long wings, I saw a blue, wide sky all around. My mind started to teeter, the dizziness returning, but then it cleared.

I saw a golden palace at the top of a mountain of clouds. We flew around the palace, low where the clouds puffed out and away. When we passed through the clouds, white specks of mist clung to my arms and my hair which was long and loose now from the braid Aeson had made, whipping out from my head.

I looked up. The raven had a sharp straight beak. The rest of him was soft. Bits of dark down flew away from his neck like black snow. He shimmered. Though he was still one of the strangest things I'd ever seen, having captured me and taken me away, I was not afraid of him. He held me gently in arms that were separate from his wings. I remember how he had perched on the old man's shoulder, how he had stayed so still, staring at me. The old man had ordered him to take me. The raven, it seemed, was not the one in charge.

The tall metal pillars of the palace gleamed like alien jewelry. Sky jewelry. Many rooms of the structure were open-roofed. Some looked like wall-less, suspended patios. I could see inside the huge main hall. People in white chitons stood on black and white checkered marble floors. Courtyards jutted out and led to floating gardens of furred green plants and flowers of every hue like bright eyes watching me. All of it was bathed in the sunlight which was like clear, pale liquid. Everything swam in it. Dripping.

All the people looked wealthy, youthful, shining. Some were obviously servants, heads bowed, naked, but they still glowed. As we drew closer, I could see some were not human. Several men had ram's horns on the sides of their heads. There were child-sized people with small, decorative wings jutting from their backs. None of them looked remotely like the large raven who'd brought me here. Many of these strangers looked up as the raven circled, entered through the open rooftop, and finally landed on the checkered, main hall floor. His arms set me down; he pressed a silken wing against my naked back.

I could not catch my breath. Dizzy, I fell forward. Through the wine-light, I saw only the black and white tile before me, and inhaled the scents of the bouquets of the place: orchids, myrrh oils, held-back rain.

I was stunned, braced on my hands and knees. My hair draped like a veil about me. I breathed fast, trying to orient myself.

"Ganymede, rise." The voice boomed. It was not the relaxed and calm tone of the raven, whose embrace I wanted to return to, but familiar still. This was the voice of the old man with the crooked staff who had made the deal with my father to take me away.

I felt a severing pain at the still-fresh memory. A crease in my mind. Tears sparked from my eyes.

The soft raven's touch—an edge of wing—nudged at my waist. I moved my torso up until I sat against the backs of my heels. Strands of long bangs stuck to my face. My breaths came quicker, the tears fiery on my cheeks. I could not clearly see.

"Bring him forward," said the voice.

Blind with sobs, I felt the air move. The raven had me in his embrace again, within those dark arms that extended from somewhere underneath his wings. Those arms pulled me to my feet. I wanted to turn into him, burrow into his down. I wanted him to take me home. Or somewhere where it was just me and him.

"Look up. Look at me," said the powerful voice.

I gazed up through water and salt. With blurred vision I saw a large white throne occupied by a well-muscled giant of a man with shoulder-length black hair and a youthful face. He had a fresh garland of laurel circling the crown of his head. Surely this could not be the same old man who'd stood by my father's side. Yet his voice was the same. And the image of him growing younger just before the raven took me from Tros was the same.

Beyond the king's head were stars on a black fabric like a scarf or a flag undulating in a soundless breeze. But it wasn't cloth. It was the sky as though seen though a floating night window, though it was daylight where we were. The stars made pictures. Hunters. Dippers. Sister-witches. The window was like a hole through daylight into the night.

The raven pushed me closer to the big man on the throne. The king's be-ringed hand reached out—

I flinched away.

"Now, now," he said, leaning forward. He touched me on my wet cheek, on the rib cage of my bare chest, and my hip where the top part of my still-belted chiton draped my lower half. His fingers were smooth, gentle, his stance, quizzical.

30

They lingered upon my narrow waist. My body quivered with grief and fear.

"Little one," he said. "You have no reason to be sad. You are here for pleasure. Rejoice!"

I was not little, but compared to him, a virtual giant next to me in my powerless position, I was diminished. I tried to speak but my voice stopped in the back of my throat.

"Your family is rich now. Well-tended. You will be wealthy in your own right. And I will make you immortal. Why do you cry?"

"B-but w-why me?" I managed to stutter.

The king shrugged. "Simply, you are the most beautiful boy I've ever seen."

No compliment, to be sure for if that was what earned me separation from my family, then beauty was a curse.

"I want to go home," I blurted out. My voice shook.

"But you are to be honored. Of course you have heard of me, have you not?"

I shook my head.

"What do they teach boys like you in Tros? I am Zeus."

"I have heard of you. In make-believe stories."

"Make-believe?" His tenor, already loud, rose. Then he laughed. "You are not a believer, then."

My throat closed on any reply I might have given. But of course I was not a believer, and at that point I was still convinced he was lying. He said he'd make me immortal. I did not believe any such thing could be possible.

"I traded great wealth for you, boy. Enough that your father could not say 'no'." His eyes narrowed, though his lips curved up in amusement. His hands rested lightly on his bare knees. "On occasion, I find great intrigue in innocent humans. Once a century or so, I hunt them. I watch them through 'finders'." He raised his hand as if to brush the word aside. "You will understand that later. When I discover one that stands out to me, I take him. Or her. I do not discriminate between genders."

"Kidnap," I uttered.

"What was that?"

"It's called kidnapping, not 'taking'," I said with more force.

"That is such an ugly word. If I was a bit rough in your father's hall, I do apologize, but most humans of your era respond quicker to force and demand. Your father was no different. Besides, you must know to be chosen by me is the highest of honors. You will be rewarded again and again for it."

"But why?"

"You stand out, Ganymede. I have never seen one such as you, no greater beauty even amongst all the gods. It is even more appealing that you do not see it in yourself."

My beauty? He was insane. A zealot king gone mad. It happened all the time. Kingship seemed cursed to drive many men mad. Including my one and only father. To have sold me for some horses and gold! Zeus or not, this was madness.

I only wanted to see Cinth again. And Mik and Pal and Thon. Dymos would wander the palace wondering where I'd gone, why I'd abandoned him. Fresh tears welled at all these thoughts.

"I collect beautiful things that entertain me. It's not unusual for beings like us, immortals," he said. "I love beautiful distractions. You shall bring me wine. Warm my bed. Easy enough. Nothing to cry over. So I say the deal is done." He waved a hand through the air and two naked male servants rushed toward me, each grabbing one of my hands.

"See to him," Zeus ordered. "Bathe him. Feed him. Whatever he needs, give it to him."

I tore away from their gentle grasps. "I need to go home!"

"This is your home now."

6. Wine from a Wall

I can never forget the many details of what followed. Pleasure, yes. More crying. No one hurt me. Not physically. But when you are made into a doll, when you are dallied like a thing with no soul, no heart, you are not fortunate, you are not rich. These were my initial thoughts.

That first day upon my arrival, Zeus dismissed me quite quickly and I was pulled along by two naked servants to a sun-dappled atrium filled with bathing pools. Fountains erupted at a touch from marble walls. Green ferns feathered the air. The servants pulled my chiton from me. As one knelt to un-do my sandals, something fell from the folds of my clothing.

I was still crying, but I could see. It was the book Cinth had given me for a naming day present. "Don't get that wet!" I commanded.

As I scrambled to retrieve it, the servant who took my chiton picked it up, holding it away from me. He said, "I will place it on the bench."

I wanted to escape them, run without looking back. But there was nowhere to run to. There was only the palace surrounded by clouds and sky, and the strange people who inhabited it. Were any of them even human? And where had my raven gone? He had been the only one who comforted me, the only one who showed the slightest concern.

My servants looked human. They were both dark-haired and perhaps three to four years my senior. Everything about them looked human enough, and like Zeus and the raven's voice in my mind, they spoke to me in Greek.

One of them pushed me under a wall fountain and I stood until I was soaked head to toe. The water came out warm, straight from the wall like magic, the air misty around me. It smelled of wet leaves and summer rain. Fresh and soothing. For the time I was under its spray, my tears calmed. My muscles unknotted.

A servant handed me a white packet that disintegrated on my palm in an aroma of lavender. Soap. I used it all over my body and in my hair.

After I was done, the servants led me to a pool of cooler water where I rinsed. One of them sat with me on an underwater bench. The other brought me a chalice of red wine. I did not realize until then how thirsty I was.

The servants themselves had beautiful bodies. I could not help but notice their chiseled physicalities, strong muscles, ample genitalia. Their backs arched beautifully as they worked. Their buttocks clenched tight as they bent, straightened, turned. They were not harsh with me, but they were not friendly, either.

I missed my raven. I had traveled far with him, and heard him speak in my mind. He was more a mystery to me than all the rest of it. Even Zeus was not as much of a puzzle for I still did not believe he was more than a powerful, glorified king. Yes, the palace was unlike any I'd ever seen. But the raven was the being my mind could not fathom. He'd flown me here over a long period of time without rest. He could be man-sized or small, and he had arms underneath his wings. What manner of creature was he?

I put the chalice to my lips and took a long drink. I don't know how long I'd been without sustenance. The warmth of the wine surged down my throat, settling like fire in my belly. The taste was tart, like unripe cherries on a salted breeze. It made me thirstier and I downed all of it.

The drink went to my head quite quickly. The pool glimmered with green light at the edges. It lapped my body with cool kisses. Sweat broke out on my brow. The servants must have noticed. They came to me and helped me up the watery steps, drying me with absorbent white cloths that smelled of sun-warmed grass.

They had allowed me to keep my gold arm band and my rings. But they insisted on bedecking me with more jewels: a gold-framed emerald on a necklace, a gold wrist-cuff carved with wind-blown leaves, and more rings so that every finger was adorned. They wrapped a pale, blue silk sash about my hips. It was merely decorative and covered little, the long ends dragging against my thighs. I tried to take it off.

"I don't want any of this!" I insisted. My head spun. I was drunk, but not too drunk to accept my new reality. I began again to sob.

One servant gently held my hands to my sides while the other finished grooming me. He trimmed my hair without taking away its length, then took some sort of foam from a glass jar and rubbed it into my scalp. He carefully combed out the tangles and arranged the now shining locks on my shoulders. Next, he took some oils from some pots on a tray and rubbed them into my skin until I smelled clean and faintly sweet. My skin glowed. He paid close attention to my face, rimming my eyes with something blue and powdery. Though my sobs had subsided, I kept blinking back tears and failing. He had to wipe at the moisture and redo the job three times. "Tut tut," he kept saying as he worked. "Shhh."

It was little comfort.

A third servant appeared and brought more to drink, different from the first drink, thicker, a liquid like melted rubies that caught at errant angles of light. I took the chalice, holding tightly to its leaf-carved, metal stem. The first serving of wine made me feel uneasy in my stomach, as well as drunk. But it took the edge off. But when I drank this, something about it filled me up. Abated my hunger. And the taste was amazing.

My skin grew warm, tingly, overly sensitive.

This wine had a different flavor from any I'd ever known, earthy like the smell of autumn and cool dark skies, but sweet and cloying. It calmed me. It took away the tears that had caught and collected in the back of my throat.

I held out the empty chalice to this third servant, who was standing idly, watching me be primped, and said, "More."

He took the cup and went to a shaded alcove where I saw a buffet-like counter topped with bottles of amber, azure and fire-red. There was a ceramic bowl with a long metal snake attached. He touched the snake and pink liquid poured from its mouth.

When he brought me back my drink, I asked, "Is it really venom from a snake?"

He looked at me strangely. One of the other servants said something in a language I did not know, and all three laughed.

Was I drinking poison?

The one who was working on my face said, "Do not worry so. You've been chosen by Zeus. If he'd wanted you dead he would have manipulated you into a battle and watched from afar. Poison is such a boring way to die."

"But what manner of snake—"

"What snake?" asked the one who'd delivered my drink.

"The metal one over there." I pointed.

He smiled. "That is a faucet or a spigot, you might say." He seemed to be struggling with the words of my language. "Your time period must be far in the past."

"What do you mean the past? We are all in the same now."

The servant who had held my hands down when I'd tried to take off my sash, said, "The spigot is like your cock. Only manufactured."

I looked at the contents of the chalice, horrified.

The man in front of my face dabbed gently at my lips with something smooth and creamy. "Quit teasing him. It's not semen, Ganymede. Or snake venom. It's a wine spigot. Like a fountain. Like the fountains you stood under to bathe in only with a longer apparatus. There's a stockpile of wine in containers in the wall. It comes out when you turn the spigot on."

My cheeks heated. "I've just never seen that before." I clenched my teeth, turned my head. Water came out of walls. Wine came out of walls. This was not normal.

"I know," he said. This one had the best command of my language, speaking it almost as well as Zeus had, or the raven's voice in my head. "There will be a lot of things here you have not ever seen. But if you're going to be cup-bearer and bed-warmer to Zeus, you're going to have to learn to use the spigot."

They all laughed as if it were a big joke.

His words made me wonder. But only for a moment. Truly, I did not care. All I wanted was to go home.

7. Prepared for the King

The servants, three of them now, took me from the baths and led me down a long, shining hall.

"I have to get my parchments." I tried to pull away from them, but the wine had gone to my head again.

"That little book you were carrying?" one of them asked. "It is safe."

"I want it."

"It will be brought to the chamber where you are to reside."

I saw again Cinth's dark form, hair curling in the wind-blown, loam-scented fields as she hunted me in our secret games. Over the years, we played outside in all weather, storm, heat, rain, wind. Games of hide and seek. Games of mischief. Sometimes we lay hand in hand in fallow grasses among the thorny asphodels and stared at the rolling, endless sky. Cinth had wanted to run away and become a riding-servant or page to any decorated warrior who'd have her, she told me. She insisted she might dress and pass for a boy. Our father allowed her to train at the sword and at twelve she'd become faster than any of us had at that age.

"You'd leave me and Dymos behind?" I'd asked her. I couldn't imagine wanting to do that myself.

My restless little sister never answered.

Her gift of poems—I could not lose it. It was all I had left from home now.

I would have had more immediate thoughts of escape, but the wine made me stupid. And from what I'd seen of the palace from the air, it was surrounded only by cloud, not land or sea. One could not walk on clouds to get away. My only conveyance had been the raven, and he was nowhere in sight.

Despair made me as stupid as the wine. It overwhelmed me. It was a devouring monster with endless heads.

The bright hall abruptly ended at a set of tall wooden doors intricately carved with wooded scenes, glades of satyrs, nymphs, dryad trees with faces, men like the ones I'd seen on arrival with ram's horns at their temples, birds with human heads, humans with bird heads. The doors opened onto a huge, luxurious room, the roof missing, everything exposed to the sky, light streaming from all directions. Despite my state of captivity, I was in awe.

The room held life-sized sculptures of horses, some bare, some mounted by men wielding thunder-bolts. The walls were not white, but painted a faint yellow, orange and teal, like perpetual sunsets captured and tamed. There was a wide, floor-to-ceiling-less window on the farther wall, the open frame ivy-embraced, and white silk flowed along its sides and curtained to the floor where it coiled and curled against marble tile and fur rugs. I could see the opening led to a stone balcony where more green plants sat in pots on ledges. There was a table and chairs out there, all of black, curving metal. A loose bouquet of flowers lay upon it.

Against the opposite wall, but facing the window, was a huge bed, red-covered and overflowing with silver, gold

38

and black pillows. A shelf with strangely bound books, not parchment scrolls, jutted from the head of the bed. On top were jars of candles, all flickering behind glass dyed pink and gold.

So much light, so much air, so much space.

I had had a prince's quarters in my father's palace, but less than a quarter the size of this room, and usually dark because my room sported only one casement with heavy, wood shutters that remained open only in the summers and still provided only a tarnished light that never reached all the corners. I relied on light from the hearth, oil lamps, candles.

The servants pushed me further into the room.

I turned to them. "This is where I will live?"

All three nodded.

"This is to be my room?"

The boldest of the three who had painted my face gave a friendly laugh. "No, you silly human. This is Zeus's room. You are to reside with him."

My heart seemed to cease beating. My gaze went to the checkered floor, fur rug-covered floor. Why had I ever thought, for one moment, that I'd be given anything? I did not even have clothing to call my own. A single long-tailed sash did not count. Although it was more than the servants themselves wore.

"You are to stay here now. The doors will be locked. But if you need something, you may press this green button." He gestured to the wall by the door where there was a frame as if for a picture, only inside the frame was a shiny, sleek black stillness showing nothing but a starless night.

I walked over to it to get a closer look. "I press down on the green circle?"

"Yes. That's right. Try it."

I reached out to the smooth surface. The green light swirled under my fingertip. I pressed but felt nothing happen.

"That's it. It feels your finger's warmth. You are done. That will call someone immediately to you." He turned away then, as if bored, but I could not stop staring at that the strange framed picture.

The servant continued. "Are you hungry? There is more wine on the table there. Don't worry about working a spigot. It's in a decanter."

The last time I'd eaten any food had been at my naming day feast. But the thought of food like that now only turned my stomach. I was, however, thirsty for more wine. "Do you people even eat food here, wherever here is?"

"Of course," he replied. "Food is great fun."

"But what about meals?"

"Food is not sustenance for us here. Food is for pleasure. Food is for games. As long as you drink the wine, you will never again need food for sustenance here."

"You live off wine?"

"It has all the nutrients you need," he replied cryptically.

I gazed toward the balcony where light streamed so gold it was almost painful. I heard the servant, on soft bare feet, leave. The doors clicked. A tiny sound. Little more than a tap. And yet it felt like a blow swung full-force that was the end of my world. That click hit me with the strength of ten men.

I went to my knees on the hard, cool floor. Tears thickened in my eyelashes. My thighs gleamed as I pushed up to my knees and crawled like a child to the balcony. There the light was white but gentle. My body stopped shivering. My skin warmed.

Again, I wondered where was my raven who'd promised to protect me? Had his words been lies? Was he just one more servant, Zeus's pet doing his bidding without question?

I sat on the floor of the balcony as close to the dark metal-worked railing as I could. Through curls of metal, I saw overlapping sky and clouds. I was on an edge of a surface, like a cliff suspended in air, trapped in nothingness in a palace that only a dream could make sense of.

I listened for a long time to the silence of the air. It touched my face in the tenderest of breezes. I thought I might hear sounds from the throne room or courtyards, or the gardens I had seen that jutted from the roofless halls. But there was nothing but the stillness of my new captivity. My young life was just beginning.

I went inward in my mind. The wine helped with my languor. I swayed with thoughts of home. I could almost smell the asphodels.

Clutching my knees to my chest, I fell asleep in the endless, sparkling daylight.

Waking was like coming down a long tunnel to an ending I feared. A voice said, "Ganymede, rise."

I knew that voice and cowered as I opened my eyes and lifted my head.

Zeus, even more beautiful than before, stood before me in a white skirt that stretched at his muscled thighs. He was smiling. He said, "If you want to sleep, we do have beds for that sort of thing. Nice and soft. Are you still tired from your travels?"

I nodded, still hazy.

He held out his hand to me, as if it were all a normal scene, as if he'd known me for years and had not just taken me and imprisoned me in his world against my will.

I got up by myself and did not take his hand.

"I see you do not trust me. It is all still strange to you. But that will change with time. You have anything you could ever want here. Anything."

"I don't even know where 'here' is." My voice came out surly. Despite my shyness, something inside me remained bold.

"You will learn. You have all of time now, and you don't even know it yet."

I didn't know what that meant. Nor did I care. All I wanted was to lie down.

Zeus led me to the big bed. He reached for me again, but I would not allow his touch. He raised his eyebrows, sighed, and pulled aside a red coverlet, moved some pillows, and indicated I should lie down.

I stared at the bed. His bed. I hesitated. I had seen him gaze at me. I was used to the nudity of others and of being nude. I did not feel awkward so much as assessed. Judged.

He took a step back. "You are beauty incarnate, Ganymede. So much so my eyes ache to look upon you. My servants did well preparing you. You should never hide your beauty. Never question it. I do not. And I place you in a position of honor here in my court. Cup-bearer to the king. And warmer of my bed."

I slid into the bed, hip first, flushing at his words. I settled easily. The bed was the softest, sweetest embrace. The pillows were plump but with a give to them that cushioned me perfectly. Again, I wanted to cry.

Zeus went to the other side of the bed. "I will rest beside you. I will not touch you," he said.

Strangely, I was not relieved at his words. I felt him get into the bed, shift, stretch. I was facing away but that made me feel even more vulnerable, so I pulled the coverlet to my waist. A sandalwood scent on the pillows calmed me. I said in a whisper, "What exactly is a cup-bearer?" I ignored the reference to warming his bed, for I knew what that meant.

I heard him inhale. "You will flank me at all times I ask for you. Sit at the foot of my throne. Hand me goblets of wine or ambrosia. Or anything else I ask."

"Anything else." I did not speak the words as a question.

"Yes. It is not difficult. A simpleton could do it."

"A simpleton."

"Yes." I heard a chuckle in his voice.

"Do you care about minds as much as beauty?"

"I used to."

They were all so cryptic here. The servants. Zeus the king. Even the raven's voice in my head, soothing as it had been, had revealed little explanation of what was happening to me. I wondered where he had gone. I had not expected to feel so bereft at his absence.

"What about intelligence?" I asked. "Wisdom?"

"Too much of that loses the poetry of the heart. I grow bored. Then I see a beautiful boy lying naked in a meadow, filled with wonder and newness, and I am quickened again."

"I'm a man, not a boy."

"Yes. You are eighteen now. But to my eyes you are still wet from your mother's womb."

"That's the olive oil your men rubbed on me."

Zeus laughed until I flushed, realizing he'd not spoken literally.

But I felt only tears well up again. I did not want to be funny, or a cup-bearer. I did not want to be in Zeus's bed. But why did he have to be so nice? He'd been so evil in my father's hall, so demanding. I vowed if he touched me I would fight him. I would yell and claw and bite.

I sniffed, wiping away damp blue powder from my eyes.

Zeus said, as if from a muffled world far from my perception, "No harm will come to you. Sleep, little one."

Still feeling drunk, I closed my eyes and let my mind go.

*

I woke weeping. Zeus was not in the room. I remembered nothing of him in the night, not his heat nor his presence except as I fell to sleep. I had no clue how long I'd slept. I had no memory of when he'd gone. The wine had left me bereft and sad. Then opening my eyes in the strange bed and remembering—it was all too much.

I'd never see Cinth or Dymos again. I missed my laughing brothers. The yellow meadows, the palace, the baths. My own rooms. My home.

I sat up, wiping my face. It didn't help. My fingers came away wet with clumped gold-blue dust.

The other strange thing was that usually upon waking I needed to void my bladder or bowels. I had had no urge to do so since my arrival.

The bed's coverlets were like wind against my body, light and airy and free of nits. Everything smelled of endless spring, dew, lilac, moss. My body was none the worse for wear, considering how long I'd traveled, how I had not really eaten, and how devastated I was. I felt strong, wide awake, clear-headed. Zeus had not hurt me. And yet I could not stop crying.

After awhile, the big wooden doors opened inward to the room, and three servants walked in. They were the same three who had served me in the baths and brought me wine.

The one who seemed to be in charge had violet eyes and long, flowing dark hair. He was well-muscled, shorter than I, but strong. He came straight to the bed, put a hand on my naked back and said, "Come." He gave a little push.

I got out of the bed and followed them into the hall and back to the baths. They worked my body again as they had before, scraping, cleaning, and this time shaving. I had no body hair left except for my eyebrows and scalp when they were done, and half an erection that embarrassed me.

They smiled at that, making me cry again.

"You can see why he is chosen," the leader said. Then he pushed me into the cool, sparkling water, palest azure in the streaming light, its little waves lapping the pool sides at my entrance. The splashing water echoed softly in the high, ceiling-less room.

I soaked for awhile, sobbing off and on. Again, one of them brought me wine in a goblet that looked worked from pure gold. I realized my mouth was salivating heavily before I had had a chance to bring it to my lips.

When I drank this time my head spun with stars and the sweetness of it filled me up and up. I drank fast, craving it quite suddenly.

"That's good," said the servant, slowly washing my hair, pouring water over the back of my head from a metal pitcher.

My skin tingled. Under the water my erection grew. I finished the wine and asked for more. My tears had slowed. I was content to bask for now, and not think. More wine came. I entered a hazy space, floating on an amber sea of light, and it seemed there were faraway voices that sounded like my brothers and sister. I could smell the baths of home, more tart and acrid than the ones of the floating palace. In that molten sea of my mind I saw shapes form. Lions. Horses. Bears. Birds. I saw all at once images of yellow flowers budding, blooming, wilting. Gold-drenched moons rose and fell. Errant sounds curled about me. A voice said, "...hand of the immortals..." Another, "...what you will do with the gift..."

Shaking me from my stupor, the servants, who had yet to offer me their names, helped me from the pool. Again, they rubbed sweet oils into my skin and dusted my eyelids.

One held out a small metal chest. Shattered emeralds and diamonds shone from the lid.

"From Zeus."

He opened it and heaps of jewelry lay tangled within. The other two took items at random from the chest and decorated me in the king's gifts. Ankle bracelets, necklaces, rings of gold with precious stones "mined from the shriveling stars themselves," one told me.

Lastly, a red sash wrapped my waist, accentuating rather than covering my exposed body.

The leader touched my cock, which had gone flaccid again since the soaking. I smacked his wrist in sudden anger.

"Those presented to the king as you are to be should show adoration in all ways."

"I have no adoration." I pulled back from them. "And we're done here." But when he said those words to me, I realized the entire palace was a testament to sensuality with wine and flowers in every room, the golden air of infinite days, and powdered, gleaming bodies mostly unclothed where even the servants remained in half-aroused states. Ivy, trellises, balconies, baths. The palace was built around them and, of course, Zeus's heavy throne. Then there was the fact that he'd stolen me for my beauty. The expectation was that I would be integrated in this field of play. For now it seemed I was a decoration in training.

The servants shrugged at my almost-attack and did not continue to touch me. They led me down more vast halls until we came into the throne room where sculptures were so tall they seemed to leap off their pedestals, and music curved the air from an unseen source.

People lounged everywhere, on pillows on the floors, or on puffed couches of white splendor. Some of Zeus's court were clothed, some not. All eyes set upon me. I was used to palatial luxuries, being paraded about for the attention of others. I was, after all, a prince. But this was luxury like I had never known. And I was among strangers, and even with refills of wine, my skin drew up in tight shivers. Nervousness closed my throat. My vision swam.

Zeus beckoned me forward and the servants gently pushed me to the steps that led to his seat. I knew I should kneel, bow my head. I had been taught all manner of royal behavior. But he had taken me against my will, and a part of my mind that was not completely exhausted, bewildered and grieving refused.

A tall man with hair blonder than mine stood a few paces away from the king. I noted he had wings thick with feathers that matched the silvery hue of his hair. He wore a leather skirt and sandals and watched me as closely as Zeus.

46

His skin was a shade lighter than the leather, and eyes like green fairy-light lit his gaze.

Zeus had told me he collected things of beauty. I wondered if this man was another one of his captives. He was far more beautiful than I, I thought, except for a chiseled, hardened demeanor that was almost off-putting.

The servants pushed until I was at the edge of the first throne-step. Zeus smiled as I stood before him; he had teeth whiter than any I'd ever seen on a man. "Ganymede, you are rested?"

I opened my mouth to answer but my voice was lost. I took a few hitched breaths.

"I can see that you are still troubled. It will take you some time to settle in, I'm sure."

Everyone was watching this exchange. The walls, the floor, the couches and banners and people all shimmered. I blinked and knew the tears again messed with the eye powder the servant had so meticulously applied.

Zeus turned his head slightly to the beautiful winged man. "Do you see now what I have been saying, Eros?"

The winged man's eyes hardened, looking me up and down. His head tilted and he gave a reluctant nod.

I looked around me but my raven was nowhere in sight. I had hoped--

Zeus rose and descended the steps until he was by my side. Without asking, he took my hand and led me up to the throne. "Sit," he commanded, and helped me into position on his throne, my legs curled beneath me. He leaned on one arm of the great chair and said, "You look fine sitting there. Just fine."

I bowed my head, my ribs pressed against the other arm-rest. My left hand gripped the edge of my sash. The other I pressed again and again to my eyes.

"Time is all you need, and we have plenty of it," he said to me. He laughed. I saw him glance down at the servants. "Bring entertainment, revelry," he ordered. "And of course more wine!"

They scurried to obey. The music grew louder. The people all around the gallery began to talk. I remained very still and tried to ignore it all, but I was curious. Homesick, I did not care about where I was, and yet I had so many questions. The mind, when confronted with the strange and the new, can't help but demand a context.

My eyes took in first the black and white checkerboard floor, and then my vision expanded, as if beyond my will, to take in potted plants, sandaled feet, bare feet, couches, people, far corridors beyond pillared doors facing the center so that I could see into them. The entryways led to ornate gardens, fountain rooms, balconies large enough to hold a dozen tables where it looked like people were playing games of dice, knucklebones, and cards.

A gold goblet was forced upon me. I drank. The wine filled me up again and I realized I'd been craving more since the baths.

It never occurred to me to be honored to be sitting on the throne of Zeus, Lord of the Air. I remained mortified, and would for a long time, as I slowly took in detail after detail of this alien domain.

8. A False Star Orphaned

Every time I glanced at Zeus, his eyes sought mine. My breath would catch in my throat. He looked so powerful, handsome, huge. I instantly turned my gaze to the main floor where the musicians had come out of wherever they'd been hidden. They played beautiful, bell-like music on lyres, flutes and other instruments I could not identify. There were nude dancers who simulated erotic acts. I'd seen many like them before in my father's court.

Bored, I looked away, holding my cup to my lips and letting the coolness of the metal rest there. I sipped the wine slowly, feeling it ignite my veins. I wanted to drink it fast but forced myself to hold back. It was already hard enough to maintain a clear head in my overwhelmed state.

Zeus watched with half-attention. He looked preoccupied. He wore a dark blue chiton today, and had his hair tied back with a black ribbon.

The blond man with the wings said, "He is making you wait."

"I am aware," Zeus replied, frowning at him.

At first I thought they were discussing me, but neither glanced in my direction. I had so many questions but now was not the time to speak. I sensed a tension in the air. All the merriment was meant to cover it.

Suddenly, Zeus clapped his hands. The musicians paused, as did the dancers. "Iasos!"

A man came from the balcony, striding gracefully through the crowd. His dark eyes flashed. He had wavy brown hair decorated with beads, and wore a fur-skin about his waist that draped against his hips and thighs.

"Sing something soothing. There is an annoyance in the air today. And my new bed-warmer is upset. Please us with your unique voice."

At Zeus's mention of me as "bed-warmer" I jerked back. I didn't look at him but I felt his gaze on me.

The man Iasos met my eyes, brows narrowed, then bowed deeply. He said something to the musicians in a language other than Greek. A dulcet tone rang through the hall. Another joined it. Eerie. Soaring. Breathtaking.

Iasos began to sing in Greek, his voice like a bell on a clear winter's day. He was cold, precise, starkly alluring. The words of the song described a boy who lived forever, whose beauty never faded. Though he was eternally young and wise, the envy of all, his thoughts became stale and repetitive to him. His reflection in the mirror disappointed him because he could not be more than he was. Eventually his body faded away, still aware. The song's ending line was: *Vanishing, a false star orphaned in time's forgetful wine.*

It was stunning. Like nothing I'd ever heard before. My mouth hung open.

Behind me, Zeus let out a quick breath. "Dour."

"Apologies, Majesty." Iasos bowed low, his hair falling forward, but he was not chagrined. A tiny smile curved the edges of his lips. He obviously knew a voice such as his could never elicit disapproval. So strong it was. The chamber still echoed from it. He looked up through wild bangs and straight at me. I thought I saw him wink.

I could only watch, frozen in shock as he strutted through an admiring crowd and disappeared beyond an open door into one of the sunlit gardens.

"What did you think, Ganymede?"

I turned. Zeus was half-draped against the edge of the throne's back, his hand gripping the top where real, fresh flowers garlanded the curves. Petals crushed under the pressure, and a sugary scent released into the air.

I wasn't sure how to respond or what was expected of me. Finally, I decided on honesty. "It was hard to breathe...hearing his voice."

"Iasos has many accolades and awards. I found him on a dying planet called Lyros more than two hundred years ago."

My eyebrows rose. "That seems not possible." And yet here I was on a floating island in the middle of clouds having been brought here by a giant raven. I was surrounded by people who were beautiful and young, some with horns, some with wings. Everything here was "not possible".

Zeus smirked. "It would seem so. But truth can be stranger than even wild imagination. You have much to learn, Ganymede."

He kept saying that, but he had offered very little information so far. I did not even know where to begin. My mind swam with wine. With shock. Softly, I heard my voice, broken but still alive, ask, "What is this place?"

"Olympus, of course." He seemed pleased that I was talking, his upper body leaning closer toward me with interest.

"There are people here who are part animal?"

"We are all animals, are we not?"

I thought of my raven again, how he had spoken in my head. I looked out over the hall, then back to Zeus's strong face. He watched me, intent. I said, "But animals are mute. And they don't have civilization."

"Animals speak in their own languages. But these people here are all from different places and civilizations, different planets."

"From a star?" I only knew the word planet as referring to points of light, stars, not places one could actually be from.

"Your planet, Earth, and its sun, both look like stars from other vantage points. But it is a round ball floating in space."

"Round? But it is a flat surface. There are edges to it, like here on Olympus. It is not a ball." I was arguing with a king! But I didn't care. I had not asked to be here. Why should I ever respect the man who stole me from hearth and home? And I was, after all, a prince myself.

Zeus smiled. "Sweet boy, it is time you learned your world is not flat."

I took a shaky breath. It was a heady concept but easier to welcome into my mind than everything else that had happened since my naming day feast. I started to speak again, but a gong sounded from nowhere and everywhere. My entire body jolted at the loud sound.

Zeus looked up, smiling. About two paces from the throne something shimmered on the air. A human-sized form took shape, yellow and pink at the edges with a pale green center that darkened and clarified before I could blink. The man who now stood before Zeus wore a long, emerald green robe that shone like a light itself. He had dark braids that brushed the floor, and a mustache that trailed by each side of his mouth like two snakes, black, limp. It touched the bottom of his chest, it was so long. On his head sat a square, tasseled hat or crown, also green, and it looked like it might fall off if he moved his head. Parts of him remained transparent. I could see the checkered floor through the bottom edges of his gown.

"You're late," Zeus said.

The man did not bow. Like me, it seemed, he did not respect Zeus. Was he another captive, perhaps? Or just an old friend?

"So easily annoyed," the apparition replied.

"Ganymede, this is Yuanshi Tianzun, the Jade Emperor, Heavenly Master of the Dawn of Jade of the Golden Door."

"I see you have been kidnapping new beauties?" Yuanshi Tianzun said. "And you can call me Tianzun, young one." To my astonishment, he bowed toward me, something he had not done to Zeus.

Zeus straightened at my side. "I paid for him a fair price."

"You stole him. You may rule your 900 worlds in your own way, but on the 900 worlds I rule kidnapping is illegal. Five hundred to one thousand years imprisonment for immortals."

"I know your law. You made that law because you were furious when your daughter fell in love with a human mortal and left you."

"That human kidnapped her. You are no better!"

"I have granted Ganymede a great gift and honor."

"Is that true? Have you asked him how he feels?"

"I know how he feels. He is brand new to everything here. He will see in time that the greatest gift of all the worlds has been bestowed upon him."

I could not believe these two powerful men were discussing me. I was no one. A prince, yes, but no one mighty, the youngest of my brothers and destined to never sit on a throne. Yet here I sat on Zeus's throne being discussed as if I held some importance. My tears dried. I put the goblet aside on the right armrest and sat up straighter, paying close attention.

Tianzun tilted his head and his square crown did not move but the tassels swung, mesmerizing me. He smiled kindly. "Your taste is impeccable, Zeus. Ganymede, a beautiful name for a beautiful boy." To me, he said, "But I am sure you were not consulted. The untamed ones of us who create immortals at a whim are not always at fault. Your captor is insane, you see. His predilections are those of someone who has not completed any trials of discipline or wisdom or respected any sagacity of the ages. He operates on impulse and chaos, decadence and hedonism. His is a lawless realm. He resents any criticism, and me most of all. His armies battle mine on the far side of Vega even now. I have come to discuss terms and negotiate the return of some of my followers whom he has imprisoned for one hundred years in a realm of utter darkness, awakening their monsters within. It is cruel."

What he said sounded like another fable, something impossible. I was quickly learning that, like a dream, anything could be true here. Including two men talking casually about armies and fighting on the far side of Vega while on the floating world of Olympus the sun shone and the music continued to softly play.

"There are two sides to every story," Zeus replied.

"Can the boy even talk? May I question him?"

"You may not!"

"Does he have a mind? Has he been prepared for his culture shock? Did he understand any of what I just said to him?"

"He is still wet from his mother's womb. What would you have me do? He is only newly arrived."

The Jade Emperor made a waving motion with his right hand, as if to dismiss Zeus outright.

Instantly, I yearned for Tianzun to take me away from Zeus. To rescue me. Finally, someone who understood my plight. Who didn't act like everything that had happened to me was right or just or a gift. I liked his robe. I liked his crown and his long mustache. I liked everything about him.

Take me with you, I thought. The muscles of my eyebrows tensed as my wish screamed in my mind. *Take me with you.* The sting behind my eyes began again. Tears splashed my already burning cheeks.

"Now look what you've done." Zeus patted my head. "And he had only just now stopped crying."

"You are a thug. I cannot believe I have come here to discuss anything with you. You are unreasonable."

"I have looked at your terms," Zeus argued. "I am feeling generous. I was willing to come to a compromise concerning them, especially concerning your men imprisoned in Tartarus. But your insults—"

Tianzun interrupted. "Your compromises are like your whims. Senseless. Drunken. Always about what you can gain and never what you might give."

Zeus made a motion with his hand and a servant ran up, naked and brown, and handed him a shiny thin square of crystal framed in black. He tapped the crystal many times as if it were a magical code that might call up the creature within. "See for yourself," Zeus said. "The compromises I offer should be on your screen now."

I watched a hand emerge from the air, though the person behind the hand was invisible to us here in the throne room. The hand presented Tianzun a crystal much like Zeus's, only the frame was gold and there were handles on each side carved in the shapes of miniature dragons. Tianzun was silent a moment as he studied the crystal.

I realized that Tianzun stood in another place, maybe even another time, and that we were looking at him as if through a window where we could not see what the edges of the window obscured.

Tianzun looked up. "You will release my men if I retreat to Touching-the-Golden-Past aurora?"

"Yes."

"That is too far. I will take my bird-ships to the edge of the Realm of the Invisible City. You will stay away from the River of Stars Bridge."

Zeus grunted, tapping his magic code again. "And I want the men you have been keeping returned to me."

"They are in my realm at their own free will," Tianzun said. "I cannot force them. But I will allow them to speak to you if you return my followers to me."

"Do not lie and tell me some of mine are not your prisoners!"

Ignoring the statement, Tianzun said, "Do we have a deal?"

Eyebrows narrowing, Zeus paused. Finally, he sighed. "We do."

"Very well." Tianzun looked up from his dragon-crowned crystal and straight into my still-teary eyes. "And I want Ganymede."

I gasped. Everyone in the great room gasped. I lifted my head. Zeus's hand still rested in my hair. It slid very slowly back and forth. "Request denied."

I held my breath, watching to see what Tianzun would do or say. To my disappointment, he gave a half-hearted smile and said, "I had to try, now, didn't I?"

Zeus's hand tightened, pulling at my locks. "You keep insulting me today. I feel an urge to withdraw all we have agreed upon."

"Yes. Yes. I know when I have out-stayed my welcome. We will meet in person next time, yes?"

Zeus actually laughed. "Yes, and I will serve you noodles and vegetable bowls in your honor."

"It has been a long time." Then Tianzun looked straight at me. "I'm sorry, Ganymede."

My jaw quivered. My face was very wet. There was no time to even think, let alone respond, as the Jade Emperor vanished quicker than a brass snuffer extinguishing a candle.

Now I felt both of Zeus's hands on my head, cupping each side, turning me to face him. His large thumbs caressed my soaked cheeks. "Hush," he said softly. "You do not need tears. You should be in awe and amazement. You have just met the Jade Emperor and he favored you. Now you are favored by the two most powerful rulers of the galaxy. So weep no more, my beauty."

I gasped several more times, then swallowed my tears.

He raised his eyes from mine. To the room he said, "We have an accord for the day. An agreement. We shall have revelry and merriment. Anything you wish." He looked back down at me. "Ganymede, what do you want?" He quickly added, "Anything but to return home."

"I—I—"

Though I had never liked casual or overt touching, shyness had never been a feature of mine, not since I passed seven years. But now so many words seemed stuck in my throat, and my mind moved faster than I could keep up trying to invent contexts, asking too many questions at once, resulting in my stupid and confused state.

Although I could not tell time here, for the sun was always out, this seemed to be my second day. But how long I'd been in the raven's arms I could not recall. Only that I missed that softness, and his strange promise of protection. At that thought, other than going home I knew what I wanted.

"Where is the raven who brought me here?"

"Ah, yes. Excellent. Sable prefers an aerie close by, constructed just for his use. Shall I summon him?"

Sable. Now I knew his name. I nodded. "Is he small or big? When I first saw him, he was on your shoulder."

"So many words, more than I have heard from you before. You make me happy, Ganymede, that you are speaking. To answer your question, he is as big as you or I. But he can shift his shape at will. The raven on my shoulder was to complete my image only. I was never really in your father's hall to begin with. Only my image and my voice. And Sable."

Slowly, I was beginning to understand that these people could project themselves, like one would a voice, into far distances. Like an echo of a person's real self.

"Is he an animal?" I did not want to say he had spoken to me. It felt too much like a secret that I should not reveal.

"His kind are rare. They are called Solumnists. They are incredible shape shifters. Even outer space is no barrier to them. Sable has been with me for decades. He prefers the large raven form and stays to himself. He chooses not to function within our society here, but I take care of him. He is very loyal to me, and he obeys my every command."

I wondered what his real form was, for a raven was an Earth bird and he was not of Earth.

Solumnist. Sable. I kept saying the two words in my mind over and over. "I would like to see him again."

"Whatever you wish, as I said." Zeus still held his crystal window. Now he brought it up and tapped his magic code on it. "All right, that's it. He will arrive for the revelries."

At last I had something to look forward to. But also a private motive. I could not escape Zeus on my own. There was nowhere to go. But Sable could. Zeus said he answered only his commands, was very loyal, but I remembered that smooth voice in my head, the promise the raven had made to protect me. Maybe I had understood only what I wanted or hoped to hear, but Sable was the one who'd brought me to Olympus. It stood to reason he was the only one who might be able to take me home. I couldn't fight the people here and in truth they were not mean to me so I had no desire to start anything violent. And with only human strength, I could never hope to over-take Zeus. But patience was something I did have. If I could win the trust, even love of Sable, I might stand a chance of escaping.

Now Zeus faced the room again. "Bring a feast. And buckets of oil. Food. Dancing. Orgies. We shall stop only for sleep!"

A roar of approval went up from the gathered court, gaining further volume from those outside on the balconies or in the gardens.

I took a deep breath and leaned further back into the throne, not at all ready to watch this spectacle.

9. Merriment, Eros and Knucklebones

The orgies did not happen right away, much to my relief. People drank, danced and lingered. A feast was brought in on rolling tables and half the guests lined up, took plates and helped themselves. Zucchini keftedes with feta and dill, lemon-roasted potatoes, grape leaves stuffed with dill-scented rice, lamb chops with lemon, salad with papaya dressing, goat cheese with olives, polenta cake with orange blossom, walnut and pistachio baklava, and dozens more dishes.

"I ordered Greek delicacies in honor of you," Zeus told me. Only then did I realize my country's food wasn't the only kind they ate.

I still wasn't the least bit hungry, but the scents made my mouth water. I was allowed to leave Zeus's side to serve myself. I piled my plate high, came back to the throne, sat and picked at my food always aware of Zeus's eyes on me, and of the way the long ends of my red sash kept tangling between my legs.

When I'd first arrived, a banner of stars arched over Zeus's head, but tonight the image in the strange window above the throne was a grand city at night, larger than any I'd ever seen with palaces and castles so tall they seemed to scrape the stars. It looked as if ten thousand candles and oil lamps lit the city up, a monstrosity of glittering towers.

Here in Olympus it was still bright daytime; a gentle breeze blew fuchsia petals and old ivy leaves from the balconies and onto the hard, clean floor. Servants raced to gather them. I watched every opening in the grand room for the return of the raven. Sable. A being who could shape shift. A being who could fly through the firmament and up to the stars.

As the feast progressed and people abandoned their plates and cups, Zeus clapped his hands and called for a game of chess.

It seemed odd to me. Chess was a game for two players in a usually quiet room, less chaotic.

I watched as a large portion of the floor in front of the throne was cleared. Then people started lining up on the black and white square tiles. I realized now the chess game would be life-sized with live beings as the pieces. I wondered what would happen when a piece was sacrificed. Would there be bloodshed?

Naked servants played the parts of pawns. Sashes were passed to each participant. White on one side, black on the other. Some tied them about their waists; others wore them around their necks or as cowls over their heads and faces. Zeus strode to the white side. The man with the blond wings whom he'd called Eros stood behind the black.

One by one, they called their moves. Pawns first. Then more powerful pieces. I was quite fascinated by it all as I continued to drunkenly search for Sable to appear. People moved about the chess board as ordered, laughing, leaping from square to square. When they were out, they went to sit on the sidelines with no bloodshed, much to my relief.

Though hours had passed since what I thought was the morning, the light remained with the same brightness, the air tinged with summer and tranquility.

I heard the ruffle of feathers before I saw him. Odd. I had remembered him with gold eyes but today they were black diamonds, and his brilliant ebony plumage simmered with a bluish undercoat. I held my breath as he moved gracefully forward from the far left balcony, not hopping as ravens did, but walking. He was a strange combination of man and bird and I could not look away.

He tilted his head and leveled one dark eye upon me. I glanced at Zeus, still involved in his chess game—and slowly losing—then back at Sable. I got up from the throne and moved toward the bird. He stood by the sculpture of a charging stallion but moved no further to take part in the dancing, the feasting, the live game of chess.

I was surprised when all of the guests ignored him. He was breathtaking. And so very strange. I came to stand by his side, still and quiet for a long moment. Then I said softly, "Your name is Sable."

No response.

"I asked for you."

My mind stayed silent.

"For you," I repeated.

No voice spoke inside me. Had I dreamed it before? Had my journey to Olympus been so traumatic that I only imagined the raven had spoken even if only in my thoughts?

No. It had been real. He had given me commands, told me how to hold onto him and that I would sleep for a time.

"Do you even hear me?" I asked softly.

I saw him tilt his head slightly. There was a flicker in one dark eye.

For the first time in Olympus, I wanted to smile. I knew his response was for me. It was not my imagination. Maybe there was a reason he did not speak to me mind to mind at this time. Maybe he did not want Zeus to know he could.

It was odd how my body reacted to him. Standing beside him, I took my first deep breath since being stolen from my home. My tears had stopped. My muscles relaxed. I felt

60

safe beside him even though the raven had taken me just as surely as Zeus had. He'd swept me up and away from my castle, bound me tight in his strange human arms so I could not move. Even now he did not make any gesture to help me leave, and he had to know I was here against my will.

But he had made that one promise. *I will protect you. I swear it.* His soothing tone still echoed through my mind.

As long as he remained, I believed with all my heart I'd be safe.

For the rest of the chess game we stood side by side. I kept thinking about how soft he was, the way his feathers had pressed to my body in warmth and safety. I did not relish the touch of others, but I wanted to touch him. Only him.

Sable did not seem interested in food or wine. I wondered how he lived, and what he might eat if he ate at all. If he remained mute with me, I'd never know. I vowed then and there I would hear that melodic voice in my mind again no matter what it took.

At the end of the chess game, with Zeus the obvious loser, it degenerated into drunken chaos, the fake-dead, half-naked chess pieces piling on top of each other, laughing, undulating.

I'm not sure when the chess game turned from real chess and into a blatant orgy, but the pile grew as more and more guests joined in, naked or partially clothed, offering themselves or taking what was freely offered.

At first, I did not feel the least bit aroused watching oiled bodies clash, slide together, and slip apart only to join others elsewhere on the floor, on the couches, over-spilling to the balconies and halls. But as the spectacle progressed, I felt ripples on my skin, and a slow heat building.

Instead of feeling good, it only annoyed me. I turned away. But I could still hear the groans, the laughter, the urging commands of lovers giving, receiving. I could smell the lavender and orange oils they used, a thick sweetness on the air.

There was a graceful wave of lust emanating throughout the room and no way to keep it from touching me. I wanted to stay apart from it all, keep grieving, keep myself frozen and distant, time-locked in a secret place that had me dangling endlessly between being snatched from my old life and being forced to embark on a new one. This mind-space held me between victim and participant, boy and man, past and future. I did not want to move one step forward. I did not want to accept anything except Sable of this new reality with which I had been presented.

It was both easy and hard to look away. Anger and hurt fueled me. But curiosity peeked, too, and awe. A six foot raven stood by my side. How could I not be in awe?

Was Sable watching the party? When I turned my head to look at him, I saw he faced the center of the room, but I could not tell where his gaze settled. He made no motion, but stood very still. I could not even see him breathing.

As if pulled by strings not under my command, my head turned, my peripheral vision taking in the spectacle again. Erect. Open. Pushing. Sucking. Pleasure took the hall in its spell. Ecstasy. Exultation. Euphoria. A fever engulfed me as I watched from askew, and it felt as if I were floating above myself, outside looking in at the grand palace, the pleasure-seekers, and me folded in on myself, arms crossed, pale hair curving along my bare chest, eyes of tawny flame.

Light emanated from all directions, clean and pure.

"You can make yourself miserable, or you can forget yourself for a while and experience pure bliss," said a sharp voice behind me.

I turned. Eros stood close by, unclothed now, explicitly unabashed in naked splendor. He was covered in a thin sheen of oil and natural flush, slightly tanner than I, a little taller. His muscles were lean and graceful. Little white under-feathers from his wings stuck to his lower back. His erect penis pointed to his belly. He had no hair down there, and his skin looked silken. He smelled of honey. He was breathtaking. I gazed into his eyes which were a pale, summer green.

"However," he added, "you are for none but Zeus. All but his favored servants are forbidden to touch you."

Even Sable? I wondered. Was that why he made no moves toward me even to communicate?

"I don't want Zeus." My voice came shaky, though I was no stranger to talking to naked men at home in the baths, or at play when I was a child, though I had never been involved in pederasty, a common Greek custom for boys. Maybe that was why I felt prudish. More obviously, it was just the shock of it all, and everyone a stranger to me.

"You're naïve. Besides, he's the greatest lover in the four quadrants. I've had him countless times."

I had no response, and could only gaze at him in wonder. Like a sculpture, he was perfect in every way. And for a moment my mind hedged on the idea of touching him, and him touching me, those smooth arms supporting me, that satin chest against mine.

I swallowed hard.

My mind rushed. I glanced to where Sable remained at my side with a quick feeling of guilt that Eros had almost tempted me. The raven still did not move.

Eros chuckled. "Ganymede the virgin. How delightful you are with your pink cheeks and little bobbing pet awake between your legs. So shy."

The lust in my veins turned from hesitant sweetness to an outright sting. "I'm not shy. I'm sad and I'm angry!"

"I know." His face turned hard as he said it. "Everyone knows. For everyone has been angry at Zeus at one time or another. He's infuriating."

"But—"

"Soon you will see the gift he has given you. Maybe then you'll lose some of that tension."

"He took me from my home!"

Eros leaned against the stallion sculpture base. "We've all had homes taken from us at one point or another, or us from them. Nothing lasts. Or stays the same. Except here. Olympus is a grounding point, a touchstone for many of us."

I wanted to ask who "us" was. The gods? They weren't gods, were they? No, just strange people who claimed to be immortal.

"But I was taken against my will."

"I heard it told that your father sold you."

"He had no right!"

"Hmm, didn't he?" He lowered his eyes and the edges of his lashes glimmered like gilt.

I was not educated on all our laws in Tros. But from what I could remember, nothing said he couldn't. I just never thought he would.

"I wanted to come ask you to play with me," Eros said.

My gaze darted to his middle where he was aroused still.

"Not that." He waved at my head. "I've had my fill for the day. Get up from the floor. Come with me."

"But Zeus—"

"Fuck Zeus." Then he looked up just past my head. "Is the bird with you?"

"Yes. He's with me. And his name is Sable."

"I know his name. Usually he's Zeus's pet. But if he gave him to you, who am I to argue?" Eros shrugged, moving away from me, his flanks flexing in smooth perfection. I followed him, saying over my shoulder, "Sable, please come with me."

Sable moved then, following close behind. Obviously he had heard me just fine all along.

I wasn't sure I entirely trusted Eros. Much as I saw Zeus as an enemy, Eros's irreverence for the king brought an instinct of wariness I'd learned from being a prince.

Eros led me to one of the giant cloud-swept balconies. Plants and trees in pots decorated the walls. Flowers spilled everywhere, loose on the floor or growing from hanging pots: hyacinth, lotus, and narcissus. The balcony ledge had a waist-high railing wrought with designs of snakes and dragons, their tails curling about each other. Above, the sky's expanse went on and on, my blue captivity.

The raven came to stand against one of the walls by an orange tree. It did not seem as if he was watching me, but I felt an awareness of him like no one else here. Quiet. Comforting.

Eros led me to a low table with pillows all around. We sat, not too near each other, and he said, "I know you would not understand the screen games many love—"

"Screen games?"

"But here. I know these. From your place of origin." He pulled up a bag onto the table and dumped it. There were cards, checkerboards, and knucklebones. Some rubber balls bounced before settling. One went off the edge of the table and I retrieved it with a deft catch.

The game of jacks, or knucklebones, was one I excelled at. It was a familiar thing in all the strangeness. I suddenly forgot where I was for a moment, and took up the ball, bouncing it, grabbing a handful of the wooden pieces. It was as if home was only a breath away and I remembered Cinth, like me, was also good at this game. I blinked back the memory, focusing on the table.

Eros knew the rules. He was good, too. He mixed it up, making me do eight all at once at first, then one at a time. I rarely missed.

As we played, he talked, and my heart settled more gently against my chest. I no longer felt so close to tears. Sable was close by. I almost felt relaxed.

After that, we played cards, which were strange to me, but I caught on fast.

Eros asked me questions as we played, but gentle, undemanding.

"Have you ever thought about life as it is given to you, where it might seem as if you have choices all around but really you are saddled into the role you are born into?"

I studied my hand, discarded. "You mean that I was born a prince?"

"That and even your name—Ganymede."

In truth, I had thought about a lot of the things he asked while I had lain in the asphodel fields of home. Including the idea that I had been born into the time and place not of my choosing, from parents of whom I had no recollection of ever asking to bear me. I had been a rudimentary student of philosophy mainly because my teacher had been old and tired and impatient and boring. But on my own in the library, and in the fields, I was an adept at contemplation. Or, as my mother Calli would have called it, rebellion, but never beyond just thinking too much.

"I have thought often that we are put on Earth to fulfill roles. As if in a play," I said.

Eros studied me intently, then discarded.

"There are worlds within worlds, and yet it is all one." He spoke as a hierophant, a priest to me, and yet casual and naked, as if he had no cares.

"This…this is all like a dream," I said.

"Even dreams are included in the one world. Nonsensical performances on the ledge of mind's jump to new continuums. It's all one."

"What are new continuums?"

"Well, Olympus is one for you right now. Not everyone can make the leap, yet here you are."

"I made no leap."

"You are making it. Your leap hasn't yet landed. Maybe it never will."

I liked Eros's talk of deep things, but I still felt my anger rise. The sad anguish of my fate. The audacity of Zeus. "I was bought because of my looks. So that reason is beyond my choice, too. I did not earn my way here. Or anywhere."

We played more hands, taking, discarding, an ancient game of rummy from before my time.

"Zeus," said Eros, "is jaded and proud. But he wasn't always that way. He has mindfulness, too. He forgets, though, too easily, what it was like when he was a student, and the ways of patience and courting and learning. Now he takes what he wants and feels no need to explain."

I shifted on my moss-soft pillow, straightening my sash and scratching my tummy. I said, "I heard him say he rules over 900 worlds. I haven't seen him do much ruling except talk to Tianzun. He's mostly drinking."

"And fucking," Eros added, finishing my unspoken thought.

"Yes," I agreed.

"But he is a leader. You heard his meeting with Tianzun. They play real chess in space as well and for bigger prizes. He is the icon of those 900 worlds."

"900 is a lot."

"It may seem like a lot but in this galaxy alone are billions of worlds. His realm is the tip of the mountain. No, it's the grain of sand on the tip of the mountain."

"Billions of worlds? Like countries?"

"Entire planets. They are like islands in your Aegean, only this Aegean called Void is a much vaster sea. These islands orbit stars and only special ships can take you there."

"You say he was once your teacher. How old is he?"

"I said he was a leader. Not my teacher. In fact, I was his teacher once. And how old are we? The number would mean little to you. When you are as old as we are you begin to see the longer cycles, the ones mortals will never live long enough to experience. One such cycle is the necessity of losing oneself in the Lethe."

"The Lethe? The River of Forgetfulness? It's nowhere real in Greece. It's a—" I started to say "a myth".

"The rivers of the mind are vast. And very very real. But now is not the time for Lethe, for sleeping for centuries and then starting over. Now is a time of decadence on Olympus. This is one of many centuries-long parties Zeus has thrown. And you have been invited. You could surely have done worse for yourself."

His words left more questions than answers to my plight. But I beat him at rummy nine out of twelve times. For some moments I forgot my homesickness and was hesitantly grateful.

In the orange tree's shade, Sable stood, a darker shadow. That made me grateful as well. Every time I started to become overwhelmed, I would glance at him. To have him close felt like being able to breathe easy. I did not feel so completely alone and stranded as I had at the beginning of my day.

"You don't understand this gift of coming to Olympus yet. Perhaps you will never fully understand," Eros said, glancing at Sable. His eyebrows shifted. "It's funny with the bird people." He pitched his voice low. "An imprinting thing happens sometimes."

"Oh, no. That's not why he's here. I requested him."

"I know. I meant that you formed an attachment to him. The flight here was long. It happens."

"You mean I imprinted on him?"

"Yes."

"I just—I feel more at ease when he's around. Safe. That's all."

"You don't have any idea how long that flight was, do you?"

"From Earth to Olympus? Maybe a day or two?"

Eros smiled. "Maybe longer."

"How long?" A rush of fear returned to my veins.

"I will simply say that Sable is talented at the longer journeys with minimal technology required and less shock to the system of the traveler he carries."

"I did sleep. And I thought I heard—" I stopped. I didn't want to say I'd heard Sable speak. I still felt as if it was our secret.

"Heard what?"

"I dreamed, I think. I don't know." But the comfort of Sable's voice had not been a dream.

"It was your first foray into star travel, and the warp portals can surely dizzy the mind and disorient. Sable adds an organic grounding force the metal ships do not offer to passengers. He is of great value to Zeus. Zeus found him in the Broken Star Fields wounded, barely alive. No one knows how he got there, or why, but Zeus brought him here. He healed. I will say it again; Sable is very loyal to Zeus."

My heart skipped. The only ally I felt good around was Zeus's accomplice. Of course I knew this. But the memory of his voice... *I swear it.*

"Do not look so sad." Eros leaned closer to me, arms on the tabletop. "You will make friends easily here. Everyone will love you, Ganymede. You are an infusion of innocence and purity here that we haven't seen in some time."

But I didn't want to be anyone's infusion. Or sweet. My throat tightened again. Eros encouraged one more game from me, but I could not concentrate. Too much was happening too fast. And though he was good at distracting me, as if pulling my favorite subjects right out of my mind, I wasn't sure I liked him.

At that realization, my tears began to return.

Eros poured me more wine from a decanter on the table. "Drink. It always helps."

I shook my head. "I would like to sleep again, I think." I started to get up from the pile of pillows.

Eros watched me through half-closed eyes, a reclining sculpture of beauty on purple satin pillows. "You can sleep here. Sable will watch over you, I'm sure."

"I want silence." I turned away from him and looked out over the railing at clouds so white they hurt the eyes. The tears cleared my vision as I blinked. "I need to be by myself. To think."

"I'm sure if you ask nicely Zeus will have his servants escort you back to his bed."

I said nothing, just leaned on the railing and watched the clouds through blurred eyes. At some point, I heard Eros get up. Some time later, I sensed the approach of more people. I turned to look and saw the same three servants who had attended me since my arrival.

The boldest one spoke, as always. "The king is occupied. We are to escort you back to his chamber."

"Thank you. I do wish to sleep."

He nodded.

We went through the room where the orgy continued unabated, though some participants lounged, napping on floor pillows and couches. There was spice in the air, and candle flame, and the aroma of sex, salty, musky. Just one glimpse of the sea of moving, naked bodies made my skin feverish again. I saw Zeus in the center, fucking a horned man from behind. A small gasp escaped me.

Eros went straight to him, flung an arm around him and kissed him on the lips.

Burning, I looked away, my eye catching a darkness trailing behind me. I didn't realize Sable would follow me to Zeus's private rooms. But I had requested him. And Zeus said I could have him. Did that mean he was mine to take everywhere I went? I liked that idea, and yet Eros's words of the raven's fealty to Zeus, and Eros's immediate kisses upon Zeus's lips made me feel betrayed from every direction.

I wanted only to sleep and forget.

10. Sparkling Boy in the Asphodels

The servants brought me directly to Zeus's quarters. They did not detour to the baths and I was grateful. Sable followed. I was surprised but not, then a little frustrated when he did not seem interested in me in the least, and moved right past me to stand on the open balcony.

Deep inside, I knew there had to be a reason. I let him be.

I dispensed with my leaf garland, sash and some of the bracelets, and climbed into Zeus's big bed. My body was a bronze lean-ness against the blushing, sunset colors of the coverlet and pillows.

The raven stood silent, near but far. Blue where the light tried to pierce him but could not take hold. Black as if made special without stars, without light. His beak: a curved sword. His crown: ruffled night.

I said, my voice hazy-drunk, "Sable, I wish I were you."

I don't know why I said that. He was the one who'd captured me. He was the one who flew me on high. The king's henchman. The king's minion.

Still, Sable said nothing. I don't know if he even heard me.

I turned my gaze away from the bird toward the clouds and the blue-blue sky. After awhile, I looked away, the cushions next to me coming into view. The pillow nearest to my head had red fringe around a blue square of material that looked lightly furred. In the middle of that square sat a small, cloth-bound sheaf of trimmed parchments. The book Cinth had given me on my naming day had been saved. It was the only thing other than a few rings, my formal chiton, a belt and sandals that had made the journey with me from Tros to Olympus.

I reached out to caress the book, the roughness of the cover catching my fingertips. It was solid, real. A touchstone from home. Propping myself on more pillows, I picked it up and opened it to the first page.

Cinth had copied my favorite poem there, decorating it with a border of grape leaves and their cones of purple flowers. I turned page after page. Her swiftly curlicued writing scattered across the pages, along with her pretty painted borders of laurel leaves, sunflowers, starbursts and crescent moons. Most of the poems were fragments since the entire versions were epic and dozens or hundreds of passages long. She had chosen all of my favorite parts, the ones we sometimes recited together out in the wind-tossed meadows, or when we were little and lived together in the children's nursery until I was thirteen and she, seven.

On the last page, in her best hand, Cinth had gifted me with a poem of her own. Short but shining in her captured essence of me. My talented, genius, strong but tender-hearted sister.

I read it until I had it memorized.

He is sun-dazzled
in the bittersweet fields
searching the long skies
the great unknown

his symbol is the swan
graceful to rise
the first new star
his guide

prince brother
sparkling boy in the asphodels
hair of flaxen fairy gold
seeing you
the awestruck sky cheats on the sun

(postscript)
for you, beloved Ganymede
leaving childhood behind

but still ever the dreamer
on this naming day
of your eighteenth year

Sobs caught in my throat. Choked me. I clutched the little book to my chest until I grew exhausted and fell asleep.

*

There was no reprimand of wrong-doing toward me from anyone in Olympus, not from Zeus, not from Sable, not from Eros. Only a steadfast attention, such as questions:

"Why do you cry?"

"Ganymede, will you play the White King? Or the Knight?"

"Don't you realize what a gift you are to the gods?"

The servants and some guests made rudimentary attempts at inclusiveness. In the weeks I'd been a prisoner at Olympus, Zeus never touched me sexually, but continued to pet my head and shoulders whenever it suited him. When he felt like sleeping, which was far less than I slept, he occupied the other half of his bed. He allowed me to sit on his throne instead of on the gleaming stone steps in front of it. Eros taught me new games to occupy my despondent mind. And Sable shadowed my every move, even in the baths.

Though Sable appeared to show little interest in me around the palace, whether in Zeus's chamber or the throne room, he was always close. While I slept or spent time reading in bed, he stood on the balcony within view, a being without inflection, without words. Not since the flight to Olympus had he once spoken in my mind. It had been weeks now, and still he did not speak. I started to think my memory of his voice had been unreal or a dream.

But in the baths it seemed as if he watched me closely. Maybe it was my imagination. Or some awful remnant of hope still festering within me.

73

This morning I felt his attention again. As I bathed and the servants groomed me my focus was exclusively on him.

"Sable, would you like a bath?" I asked.

He appeared to be watching, but never even twitched at my question.

As I entered the cooling pool by the open wall with its vista of fluffed clouds, my skin freshly glowing with remnants of olive oil, I thought then that I saw a shift of his feathers. It was so minute it appeared as only a flicker of ultramarine, blue's essence more pure than sapphires. Perhaps my eyes played tricks. Perhaps it was a silent breeze.

I turned to gaze at him, cocking my hip, tilting my head. He had had yellow eyes in my father's hall. But here on Olympus they had always been deeply shaded night. Was this, then, the same creature who'd abducted me?

I knew the answer was yes. Zeus and Eros had confirmed it. And his presence felt the same. He smelled the same as when he'd flown me in his arms—wind-laced, slightly singed, rainy.

I spoke to him occasionally, more than just questions. But mostly when we were alone. And only when I was desperate to talk, to unload my feelings, to weep. I had grown so used to his silence, I thought if he finally did answer me one day I'd die of shock.

Standing naked on the rim of the pool, I gazed upward along the inky plumage to his left eye. The black diamond depth of it glittered. A dark light moved there. It was something. A response I wanted to believe in. An indicator that he saw me, heard me, validated me. It seemed to promise something. I knew not what. Nor how long I would have to wait.

When I entered the warm water, I was reminded as it engulfed me of his tight hold during our flight to Olympus, the way my body sank into his softness, a fresh coziness all around me. Perhaps I mistook the sensation for safety, fondness. But I had nothing left to believe in, so I hung onto that idea as a necessary truth.

The head servant, whose name I had finally learned was Nomiki, poured warm water from a crystal pitcher over my hair. His fingers gently combed a spice-scented soap through the locks.

As happened more often than not, my penis hardened in the swirling pool. It made me feel lethargic and strangely tranquil.

When Nomiki was done, he gestured for me to come out.

"I want to soak longer today."

"Zeus is expecting you."

"I don't care. Tell him that in just those words, if you wish. Make him come to me and tell me he wants me." My voice sounded irritable. I hadn't meant it, but I was tired of the primping, tired of the servants' smug faces, and just plain tired. I wanted the tranquil feeling for as long as I could have it. The wine gave it to me sometimes, but that was still different, more like power and wantonness, while this feeling was relaxation, untroubled. I welcomed it.

The three servants stood over me, staring.

Copying Zeus's gestures, I waved my hand toward them, water trailing like diamonds through the air. "Go away!"

I waited to see if Sable might react to my surliness. He did not.

The servants seemed to take my command literally. Without argument, they left the room itself, instead of retreating to the balcony or a corner fountain.

I sat up, surprised, glancing down the far hall to see if they would return. No one came.

To rest in the water alone for a change was a wonderful luxury. Alone, that was, except for Sable.

I didn't mind that he stayed. He was the only one I had grown used to having around anyway. The only one I wanted around. My protector. That was how I thought of him often, whether his promise was true or not.

I lay back in the coolness on the underwater ledge and closed my eyes. There was a fine mist upon my lips and cheeks. I took a deep breath of the lavender-scented water. It felt so healing to me both mentally and physically. I wiggled my fingers and toes. I kicked under the water feeling its silken essence cascade into and away from me. I slid further into the pool, up to my chin, and listened to the sleepy droning of the sculptured fountains that adorned all the walls. Leaves flickered out on the balcony, a beckoning green.

Sable stood by, motionless, wordless. Strangely comforting.

I moved my palms under the water and over my thighs. For the first time since my arrival, I touched myself. I rubbed my fingers against my skin lightly at first, gently gripping my erection. The flesh moved easily up and down, a little slippery in my hand, and a surge of heated pleasure billowed throughout my body. I floated to sit on the ledge again and tipped my head back, feeling the hard edge of the pool dig into my neck.

I closed my eyes.

Focusing on nothing but the warmth and the bliss, my hand moved underwater. The light cascade of the fountains echoed in the room making everything seem dream-like and secret. In the moment I was everything. I was all I had. I could just be. And I could love myself.

The pleasure was about more than how I felt physically. It was also about feeling alive. Vibrant. Real. I had a heart and some kind of spirit that made it beat. I belonged to life. I deserved life.

I used to lie in the fields of Tros in such a state of bliss. But I couldn't think of home now. I needed distance from my past self so I could just be in the here and now in the cooling pool safe and encapsulated inside myself.

My hands moved over my thighs, the hardness between my legs growing, my fingers returning to my erection, gripping fast, slow, with tenderness and with pressure. I swelled. The air throbbed. I concentrated on the dark behind my eyelids. Within it, abstract shapes of pale gray, brown and dark gold tumbled. They were nothing at first.

The water about me seethed.

Then the shapes broke apart, grew wings. A flock of black birds took flight, one of them growing closer and closer. Black-taloned. Night-sleek. A raven with plumage edged in auroras of tumultuous blues. Sea-greens. And the purples left behind when nightmares recede.

Sable stood before me in my mind, head tilted, one taloned foot raised as if to grasp some part of me, my limbs, my shoulder, my head, my—?

I remembered the journey again, and how thick his chest feathers were, welcoming and soft. Intimate. The wild-wind scent of him rushed me and my hand kept moving, kept milking, and suddenly I was coming, an endless euphoria of pulsing shadow and shattered stars.

My orgasm, even after it was finished, consumed me for many minutes.

Two things occurred to me then. One, that I was even able to feel this way after my horrendous abduction. And two, maybe Eros was right and imprinting on birds—human to bird—was a matter of fact regarding Solumnists who interacted with humans.

For a long time I did not move. I lay in a sort of serenity between waking and sleep.

When I finally did move, I opened my eyes to the clear flowing water surrounding me and the echoing cascade of the baths. There was no evidence of my emission. And I felt no guilt that it had been in baths that others might use. I didn't care if it was allowed or not. No one ever used these particular baths but me. I never even saw Zeus here.

I rose, dripping, and deliberately avoided looking at Sable out of a sudden shyness. My cheeks flamed. The servants had not returned. I found clean linens of absorbent thickness and dried myself. I left my hair unarranged, un-garlanded, and took up a red sash that had been laid out for me and wrapped it about my neck. It was so long it trailed against my buttocks behind me, and between my thighs in the front.

A golden goblet caught the light as I took it up and put it under the spigot I had learned to use. Wine splashed. I drank and it, combined with my mood in the baths, filled me with a roiling boldness. I poured a second helping, and bore the chalice with me down the shining hall, where I needed no escort, straight to Zeus's grand hall and throne room.

I heard taloned footsteps clicking behind me as Sable, still and always, followed.

11. The Boldness of the Caged

Without being guided or asked, I entered the throne room and went straight to the white-skirted Zeus, who was lounging on his throne and fiddling with a large crystal window. When I'd first arrived, he had said something about me being a cup-bearer. I thought haughtily, *Why not?* I handed him the goblet, then sprawled naked but for my red sash, now a scarf, on the steps at his feet.

Sable took up a position behind the throne, a steady shade of dark.

Zeus leaned forward in surprise, holding the goblet aloft as if it were hot or untrustworthy. "Ganymede?"

"I already drank my share," I said without looking up. "The rest is for you."

I scanned the throngs of people on the checkerboard floor. Some were openly fucking on the couches. Others played music or games. Contentment and boredom went hand in hand. But no one was complaining. Frankly, I was still in some state of awe. But I could not understand what these people did day in and day out other than waste so much time.

Zeus had continued to sleep with me sometimes, but so far had kept his distance. Except for praising my beauty in a daily ritual for all to hear, and for all to admire his impeccable taste in acquisitions of boys, he left me to myself. He demanded little.

But this day started differently. "Did the wind blow you in from some far-off balcony?" Zeus asked.

I realized my hair was still clumped and half-wet. I wore little by way of adornments, only some rings and an arm-cuff.

"Has some wild phantom possessed you?"

I replied, "If none of you ever die, how can there be ghosts?"

I heard him laugh. So what if I amused him. I felt differently today. I was tired of crying. Tired of feeling un-empowered. I wanted attention in this moment. It was heady. Made me feel like I was doing something. I liked it. Instead of hunching into myself as I had done every day up until now, I lounged with my arms and legs out-flung. Let them all look at me. Let them desire me. Let them approve. But most of all, I wanted Zeus to want me. Here and now. Why? Because I decided I was going take great pleasure in my flirting, all for the glorious fun of turning him down.

Today Eros wore a silvery robe of near-transparent cloth. It draped him in such resplendence it was difficult to look away. There was a space in the back where his wings poked through, the cool-blond feathers looking freshly oiled. His equally pale hair was pulled tightly back from his head, the ends tangling with his wings. A thin, silver-leafed semicircle crowned him.

He and Zeus were talking about things I didn't understand and it annoyed me. Stardrives and sensors and components. And something I'd heard them talk of before: DNA. Whenever I played knucklebones with Eros I would try to remember the words so I could ask him what they meant, but they vanished from my memory, as if I were blocked from not only remembering, but knowing.

"What is DN-something?" I asked them, interrupting.

Eros looked away from Zeus and turned to me with narrowed brows. "You are eavesdropping."

"What? I am right here. All Zeus does is have orgies and talk using funny words. What am I supposed to do? Close my eyes and ears?"

Zeus merely laughed, but he did not respond.

"Look beautiful, that's your job at the moment." Eros seemed to think his statement was obvious, and that it ended our talk. But I was surrounded by so many new things. If I didn't ask any questions at all, I would burst. I didn't care if I was interrupting something important right now. My new boldness had fueled me. Besides, they were no more than glorified criminals. Why should I be polite?

"What is it, though?"

"DNA. It stands for deoxyribonucleic acid. It's the building block of life."

"I don't understand."

"It's what makes you you. It forms you. Your program for your body, the color of your hair, your eyes, your skin, your size, your capacity for intelligence, health, even the tone of your voice." He got a pained look. I was sure it was because I appeared completely bewildered and could not hide that fact. But in my head I kept repeating the weird word, hoping I got it right. *Deoxyribonucleic acid.*

Eros had leaned forward on the arm of the throne, his elbows propped on the hard marble. "If you have a book with words in it and the words make a story, it's like that. DNA is your story inside you."

"It's inside me? Does it know where I'll be or where I'll go in the future?"

"No. Not like that. It's the story of how your body grows, whether it gets sick a lot, or if it might have a talented singing voice, or a big cock."

Zeus laughed again but softer, and took a drink.

"Is it the internal spirit maybe?"

He sighed. "I don't think it's exactly that. But you have much time to learn all these things. And by the way, your DNA is very special. It's one reason Zeus chose you."

"It's because of how I look…"

"In part."

Zeus rolled his eyes.

I wanted to know more. "And the other part?"

"Ask Zeus."

I glanced up at his dark visage. He was breathtaking to look at. A being of pure strength, it seemed. Zeus just gave me a little smile and shrugged. "You don't know your own greatness. No one does until they try."

It was cryptic. And a stupid answer to my mind. They were both infuriating.

Eros was sometimes a good teacher to me, but there were many times I wanted to lash out at him. He was very patient in trying to teach me things. He made wise statements. But most of the time everything he told me only elicited more questions. It made us both frustrated.

When he had tried to show me what he called the "screen-games" and made me look through little framed windows at moving things, my head ached a lot. He had pushed some buttons and a flat image of a person shot a dragon with a fiery, elongated weapon. When the dragon fell backward and died, I began to cry.

"It's not real, Ganymede!" he'd admonished.

How could I believe him? The magic window showed me beings that seemed to move, breathe, live.

After that he put the magic windows away and said when I was curious enough to ask for them again, he'd bring them out.

I had thought about them every night since, though. I wondered if the windows could show me my home again. Could I look through them and see Cinth and Dymos? I shuddered every time I thought about it, too afraid to ask.

Today as I lounged at the foot of Zeus's throne, I felt grumpy. Offended again at the very fact that these people existed who had plucked me from my home as if I were a weed they might replant and see if it would grow.

Zeus and Eros went back to their conversation. Ignoring me.

Then I heard Zeus say it again, something about "using their DNA to improve the quantum..." The words still had no meaning to me. But it seemed they were actually talking about doing something and I was so bored I wanted to be part of it.

Loudly, I drawled, "Deoxyribonucleic acid."

Zeus stopped talking and looked at me. "Ganymede?"

I glared up at him, my head tilted back. He was upside-down in my vision. "You are being rude. Talking over me. We weren't done talking about DNA. Now you're talking about it to improve something. What is it? They're building blocks, right? Are you going to build something? Armies to pilot stardrives? Some beautiful voice to sing you a lullaby at night? A duplicate of me who will want to fuck you?"

It pleased me to see Eros's mouth drop open. A few of the people nearest the throne over-heard and stopped to stare at me.

My body was hot. My head hurt. I didn't care. I didn't know why, but I wanted to make a scene. "If you can do that last thing then you can finally send me home. You won't need me here any longer."

Zeus said, "Eros, what have you been filling this boy's mind with?"

82

"Well, anything and everything. As you instructed. I didn't think he understood half of what I said even just now."

"The wine," said Zeus cryptically.

"Perhaps," said Eros. "He's more defined in the musculature. More beautiful than ever. Ambrosia enhances the brain as well. Remember it happened with you."

"Yes but I'm a god. With humans it can take years…" He trailed off, looking at me as if I were some conundrum instead of just a homesick, human boy.

"You chose him for his abilities."

"Yes, the spike in time-slip ability."

"And his blondness," Eros put in.

Again, nothing made sense. They were being crass, hurtful. I turned onto my side, gripped the sash about my neck and pulled tight in aggravation, feeling the material chafe at the skin. "Quit talking about me as if I'm not here!" I didn't realize I'd yelled until I heard the words echo about the room, causing a disturbing hush all the way to the balconies.

"It's also the decadence of this place. Your hundred-year party you won't give up. It kicks his hormones into high gear," I heard Eros casually state.

"He's not used to the pheromones pumped into the air," said Zeus, nodding.

"But he kept himself closed. Until this morning in the baths. But that seems to have just hyped him up."

At Eros's words, I jumped to my feet, hands clenched. "You were watching me?"

He gave a little smile and shrugged. That smugness reminded me in that one moment of my father, who'd mostly ignored me, but when he didn't he discounted pretty much everything I was, said or did.

"You—you--!" Tears began to sting but I didn't feel like collapsing as I usually did. Out the corner of my eye I saw Sable, motionless. Did he even care how I felt?

For some reason today *was* different, and before I knew what had come over me, I launched myself at Eros, tumbling him backward, pummeling his face with my fists.

For a moment I couldn't see. Everything was reddish, indistinct, but I felt skin and muscle, my fists colliding with it, and with Eros's pretty silver robe that I felt tear a bit just before it surrounded me, just before I hit the marble floor hard and felt his weight on me, and the closeness of his face, his breath like burnt sugar, his legs straddling me, his hard cock through the sheer material pressed against my own erect member.

I struggled but he was too strong. He held my arms over my head. My legs kicked but got me nowhere. I yelled wordlessly, then shouted, "Let me go! Sable, help!"

But no raven came to my rescue.

I squirmed beneath Eros and saw he was smiling as a single white feather drifted through the air in a lazy rocking motion to finally come to rest against the dampness of my right cheek.

He spoke, but not to me. "Zeus, control your child."

"You're doing just fine," the deep voice of the king replied, and I could hear the laughter in it.

Furious, my blind red haze only increased. I tried to rise up under Eros, his hold on me tightening as I felt his breath brush my left ear. "Ganymede, stop." I heard his whispered command through my own disjointed cries. The feel of him hard against me also sent lightning-quick shudders of pleasure through the center of my body. I felt a devastating and broken urge to come. And at the same time I wanted to strangle Eros for holding me down, for the way his body connected with mine, for his uncontested beauty that slipped and slid under that thin, silver barrier between us.

I heard Zeus mutter something indecipherable, then the word "Sable". I tried to crane my head to see if they were talking about me now. But Eros held me in place.

"You want to fight then, little one?" Eros's voice was low.

My teeth clenched on a guttural cry.

"I can teach you but you must do as I say." He thrust himself hard against my groin. I wasn't afraid of him in that manner. I was abducted by Zeus and was Zeus's alone to claim in every way. Unless the king had changed his mind without informing me.

I tried to look for Sable again, but couldn't move.

And maybe I didn't want to move. Pressed hard against me, Eros felt good.

Being held by Eros. How to describe it. In memory the mind still reels. A dance marvelous, that struggle. A wind in my veins, scented with honey. His hotness. His proud and possessing cock. His slow-moving, captivating charm. The effortless strength in gently curving muscles, softly fanning wings. The jade-glint of his eyes that beckoned. I could lose myself in that green-ness. He was, after all, the god of love. Or so he told me. But there was a sort of cold edge, too, that I did not like... or desire. Lust was one thing. I knew that from my father's own rather lascivious court on special nights when the moon went full and my brothers and I, when we were children, would hide and watch with our hands over our mouths to silence the giggles. But if I drifted too long in that sensation, that funny feeling could very quickly turn to a tightness in my belly that made me feel sick. I was a prude, yes. But also a romantic. It was the same now. If this were to happen, I wanted Eros to love me, and not love all the others, too. Not Zeus, not anyone but me. And because that would never happen, I was left with both hating my attraction to him, and not wanting to let go even in this moment of anger, of resistance. I was like a child stumbling through rocky fields to reach a river of reprieve.

I heard more whispers, and a nearby chuckle from Zeus. "Sweet baby," said Eros, licking his way past my damp cheek, meeting my lips, tongue parting them as I panted, lips fresh and petal-soft against my still-protesting mouth.

My legs no longer kicked, but I was stretched tight as a bow-string, the insides of my body knotted and wildly straining. My arms had flopped to my sides, no longer pushing. I kept crying out, "Stop. Stop." But the words never made it past my lips as Eros caught them, drank them, vanquished them. And I didn't really want him to stop. No. Not at all. But I also didn't want him to go further for three reasons: There was an audience and I was shy. There were Zeus and Sable, whom I was now convinced had been somehow communing behind my back. And I wasn't ready at this moment even if my body thought it was.

"Are you going to fuck him right here, right now, without any contract from me?" I heard Zeus ask.

Eros grunted into the sweet kissing that still devoured me.

Laughter. "He wants to kill you, you winged monstrosity."

Eros let up then, green-gazing into my wide, wet eyes. "Not anymore, I don't think." He brushed my hair back with his hand, no longer pressing me so hard to the floor.

My body went limp. The rage was receding and a slow heat flushed my cheeks, arms, legs and back. I was more aroused than I had ever been. The churning of my fury had gone into a different cycle now, but no less manic. I wanted, and did not want. Yes. No. Yes. No. Yes! The hammer of my thoughts.

Eros touched my cheek with his fingertips and brushed the white feather away. "I know," he said, voice pitched for my ears only. "But not today. Perhaps not ever. For I am not the one."

And just like that, again, I was alone, a stranger in a strange place, a boy who felt he'd lost his soul.

Wings moving like a cape about his shoulders, Eros rose. I was shaking. Damp between the thighs. Hard as a green shoot coming up from the ground in spring. Eros, I saw, was the same.

I bent my knees and sat up, hair falling along my damp cheeks, sticking to them.

I could not yet see Sable, but I saw Zeus's powerful legs as he came to stand beside me, looking down. "First lesson. You can never beat Eros. But if you want to fight, he is your best mentor. And you will have your lessons in here because, my beauty, that was the best entertainment any of us have seen in a long, long time."

I could see straight up his powerful thighs that he was hard and wanton under his skirt.

Eros scowled, his words coming sour and perhaps a bit breathless. "Happy to help." Then to my amazement, he sauntered from the hall until he was out of sight.

I hugged my scarf and brought my knees up to my chest. A servant handed me wine and I drank it all in two gulps.

I looked for Sable again. As if nothing at all had occurred, he stood still and black behind the throne.

Reality pitched and whirled.

Zeus's usual three servants showed up at my back.

Zeus said, "He was not properly groomed today. Take him back to the baths. Then to my bed chamber to sleep this off. He is too grumpy to be at my court today."

Nomiki helped me up and escorted me away. The other two servants followed, and Sable trailed behind as if this had been just another usual day at Olympus.

12. Of Fevers and Kings

I jerked from shock again and again as if awakening from a bad dream to another bad dream. In them my family lay massacred in my father's throne room, a red flood of dead bodies leaking everywhere. Dozens more, courtiers, servants—all dead.

Every time I woke and fell back to sleep, the images returned.

Finally, the bad dreams receded to be replaced by images erotic and seductive. I had an underlying sensation that I wasn't alone in the bed, only to wake in a half-daze and see the expanse of Zeus's empty bed before me, no one else in attendance except a big raven on the main balcony, his back to me.

I remember I kept saying, "What did Zeus say to you? What did he say?"

I never got an answer.

I slept again, dreaming of the king and his servants orgy-ing in raw silk sheets. Anonymous hands touched me all over. I grew impossibly hot, thrashing, waking again to see that I had spilled myself in wet pleasure all over Zeus's sheets. Instead of getting up, I moved to Zeus's side of the bed and, hugging pillows of impossible softness, I drifted into deeper, more heated slumbers.

There were times I woke to actual touches, non-erotic. Hands pressed my chest with cool efficiency. Palms cupped my fiery brow. I was rolled, gently lifted, moved to cleaner, cooler sheets. I heard the sound of water trickling into a pool. Voices. Zeus definitely. Eros, maybe. "...of internal origin..." "...river fevers, star fevers, tumults in the neuro-space..." "...no one gets sick on Olympus, it's the blood..." "...gentle now, he's half-awake..."

I had wakened, partly. I felt myself settled in someone's big arms, water lapping my body in cool relief. I shivered but liked it, wanting to submerge myself completely. I was held and the touch did not bother me but instead comforted. I half-floated, naked, in the sapphire depths of twinkling, welcoming liquid. Cups were put to my lips. I drank. It was something different from the usual wine—juices rich and trembling on my tongue from oranges, plums, lemons.

88

I revived somewhat and realized it was Zeus who held me, my body pressed to his broad chest. My hair clung in wet clumps to my shoulders and back. I blinked.

"You are feeling better," he said.

I glanced around to see we were in the private baths where Zeus's servants always took me after my sleep period. Nomiki stood by one of the fountains, ready to be called. Sable stood still and silent by a tall fern. I heard movement behind us toward the passageway back to Zeus's chamber.

"My body feels hollow," I replied, voice rough from disuse.

"You slept for a long time. Many have been worried. Even the Jade Emperor asked after you."

I moved in his arms but he held me tighter, not letting go. I realized again I was somewhat comforted by that and went limp again. "What is wrong with me?"

"Sometimes people who drink the ambrosia and begin to feel its change go to work on their bodies fall asleep for a time. Years, even. It depends upon body chemistry, origin of birth, and other factors."

"Years?"

"Do not worry. It has only been a few days. Your condition was accompanied by fever as well. And heightened libido. That is not usual. You have been well taken care of."

At his words, heat swept over my cheeks and jaw. "What change happens with the ambrosia? Have I been drinking it in the wine?"

"I told you when you arrived, Ganymede. You were to be given a great gift. Immortality. I do not give it lightly."

I took that answer for a "yes". I could not help but ask again, silently, *Why me?* But I knew he would only make comments about my essential beauty, or that he collected beautiful things and wanted to keep them forever by his side. Or maybe there was something to that DNA thing.

Now Zeus moved to stand, still holding me, effortless, in his arms as if I weighed no more than a doll made of straw.

The water came up to his thighs which I noticed were naked as he went up the steps, splashing as he came out of the pool.

He smelled of the scented waters, but also of a chilled timelessness, like the first onset of autumn in a wind that changes direction from bright south to dark north bringing with it mystery, blue silences, and a strangely delightful gloom.

I could feel that scent, the essence of him, moving through me with an invigorating yearning, an emptiness waiting to be filled.

He walked through the baths, dripping on the marble floor, still carrying me gently as he reached the corridor. He did not command towels, nor did he request the servants to follow.

For the first time I put my arms around him and held on. It wasn't really an embrace, but I saw the corners of his mouth quirk up in response. My wet thigh slid against his ribcage. My hip grazed the top of his stomach. The underside of my arm pressed the top of his shoulder, my hand clutching his neck. I lay my cheek against his flat breast, silken.

I loved the feeling of being carried, my body hot and wet against his.

We entered his chamber from the flickering, sconce-lit hall, and the sunlight gleaming there made me wince. He lifted one hand from my thigh, as if making a sign with it on the air, and something happened. The lighting dimmed. The balcony doors closed, but not before I got a glimpse of my raven, steadfast and constant, slipping through them before they completely shut. Sable, loyal to Zeus and therefore to me because I had asked for him. Because Zeus had given him to me.

Still in Zeus's arms, I looked up at him. "What did you say to Sable?"

"What? Nothing."

"No, not now. Days ago. In the throne room."

"Days ago? I do not recall."

"When I attacked Eros."

"Ah, I remember. I felt his protectiveness of you, his worry at your fury. I said his name to hold him back."

My mind reeled. Had Sable been about to intervene? And Zeus stopped him?

For the first time since being sick, I wanted to smile.

I wondered if Sable had been with me the whole time I slept fevered and nightmarish. Of course, he had. He never left me. He was always nearby, in the throne room or Zeus's chamber, the baths or the balcony where Eros and I played games.

The thought of Eros, and the last time we'd communicated, made me shiver. It was not from pain or embarrassment, and no longer anger. Just wonder. And the memory of his body holding me down, his whispers in my ear.

Zeus felt me shudder and put me down on soft sheets, my skin still damp much to my shock. He did not seem bothered at all that my body and hair were soaked. He arranged the pillows around me for my comfort, then settled himself beside me, and gathered me close.

I let him. I let him because my sensation of displacement made me feel as if I were another self. I let him because he was solid, and it seemed I'd been thinned, scattered, made into an almost-ghost by my fever. And I let him because he was gentle, undemanding and I needed that most right now. He was an unswerving presence whose touch my body was responding to with a hungering ache like nothing I'd ever felt before.

It was so unlike me.

It may seem that I too easily succumbed to Zeus, that I should have had more strength in self-denial, and definitely the stamina to keep fighting and keep hating the man who'd taken me. But in reality I was empty, and so alone. And he was powerful, beautiful and, honestly, irresistible. I later learned from Eros that I'd resisted Zeus the longest of anyone he'd ever brought to his court and fed his wine.

I'll say it again. It was so unlike me. But I was slowly becoming something else. Changed. New.

I had been intolerably hurt by my father's actions. His neglect of me in my childhood. His arrogance. His power-hungry reign. Selling me to Zeus was his ultimate crime toward me. Zeus took me, yes. But he had made an accord. He had brokered a deal and by his own laws it was just. I had been left out, given little concern to my own mind, my thoughts, my emotions. But in my culture, it had been legal. All of it.

Now I felt a concern and caring I'd always hungered for from my father, more powerful than any I'd felt before. The closest I'd felt to any manner of camaraderie with another was the sibling bond. And my playful, honest love of Cinth. The purity of that was a hidden crystal inside me I would always treasure.

But now I faced the sun that was Zeus. It nearly burned my eyes to look at him, and my heart swept up. My body filled with too much craving to contain. As if all my wishes, all I had ever wanted sped through me wanting to burst free, then scatter and forge new paths for me to wander, investigate. The Ganymede I was and who I would become stretched out in all possibility to infinity.

There was no way I could contain it.

I wanted to say, in my awkward, neophyte way, "Zeus, teach me. Tell me what it's like. Immortality? I cannot actually conceive of such a thing! Take me and train me. Edify me, spirit and mind, for I need to learn your fortitude to navigate the labyrinths of my endlessly expanding world. I must grow big to contain forever."

I didn't speak, though. In my new and sometimes frightening surroundings all words slammed into a barrier in my throat. Everything around me was a fever of illusions. Or so it seemed. And I was succumbing more and more each day.

His arms around me, powerful and hard, not forceful, but mighty, were all that seemed to hold me back from spinning off into a hundred pieces. I moved my body against his, still wet, still like a clingy child. Aroused and sure, then unsure, then sure again. Potent but held back. Fervent. Ardent. It was agony.

Voice pitched to a soothing timbre, Zeus soothed me. "You're all right. You're in the bliss. It's a wonderful and terrible thing, I know, but I will help you. You will be well cared for. Command me."

I didn't know what that meant, but it made me press tighter to him, and lock my arms about his neck.

One large hand stroked my back. When it traveled lower, over my buttocks and the backs of my thighs, lightning pleasure surged like nothing I'd ever known before. How long he stroked there, I do not know. I was burning up. Finally, his head turned on the pillows and his dark gaze filled my eyes. He was beardless today, the planes of his cheeks and the line of his jaw smooth, unblemished.

Very softy, he said my name. His breath and the word that defined my old self washed over me like a summer river. I leaned up and his lips brushed mine, the barest of caresses but I felt it over every inch of my body, as if he had a hundred mouths kissing me on a hundred different parts of my flesh. Air shuddered into my lungs. My chest swelled.

Where the backs of my thighs met my bottom, he continued to pet me. I pushed up for another kiss but he moved his head back, and the hot wind inside me impatiently wavered.

His lips moved, forming words. I could barely hear them for the thrumming pulse in my head. "Tell me 'yes'," Zeus said.

"Why?"

"Because you are not yourself."

"Who am I?"

"The emerging Ganymede."

"I'm still me."

He shook his head once, eye muscles tightening. "I do not always ask. But I am today. May I touch you?"

I gulped more air. "I want—I want—" Swallowing. Dizzy. Lifted to heights in an eroticism of coiled need. Already the ecstasy was claiming me. I could not say no.

Zeus took his hand away from my backside. I rolled, tummy up, and spread my legs; stiff between them my erection bounced on the air. I clung to Zeus's hard shoulders with my fists, then reached up and pulled tight on his thick, black hair.

His head lowered, his lips slightly parted, pink, damp. I thought of that mouth on me. I felt his own tremors just beneath the fineness of his muscle-bulging skin.

I thought of his hands and his eyes and his hips and his cock. I thought—I stopped thinking and closed my eyes. A sigh escaped me. One word. "Yes."

His hand spread over my heaving chest. His mouth touched mine. Again. This time with his lips gently moving in little embraces that squeezed my own. His hand moved to my stomach, caressing side to side.

His kiss deepened and I felt his tongue taste me. I wanted it badly. I wanted more. I pulled his shoulders down, pushed up against his hand, which moved downward, fingertips wind-like and brief along my cock until that hand came to rest, brushing my sac, cupping.

The rush might've knocked me over had I been standing. Wherever he touched I wanted more. I wanted his hand on my cock, stroking. I wanted that feral touch, that feeling of endlessness and the idea of such vitality in me, in him, so vigorous that I would never forget it.

I reached for his arm but he moved his hand up again before I could even think what to do, and his tongue invaded my mouth with a succulent burst. I sucked it in and his hand stroked up, firm on my cock, the skin sliding, the tip burning. I thrust up helplessly, groaning into his mouth. It was as pleasing as wine and poetry and sky-gazing from summer fields.

His head turned. I opened my eyes. He stroked up my cock and I reeled. My body tensed. Our gazes met. I burst free, coming in great waves, feeling the flaming liquid douse my belly and chest, the throbbings far too many to count. That was how wound up I was. That was how much I needed release, life, him. The ecstasy took me flying where everything was white and pure and fresh and I was spread upon the wind like a thing of myth. For now I existed wholly within this explicit state of arousal, this insatiable bliss.

For a brief moment, I saw a raven face staring at me, nodding. Then it was gone.

I rolled half onto my side and slid into Zeus's arms again. He murmured endearments. "More beautiful than my son Hermes. The touch of your body like a warm brook upon my skin. Ah, sweet boy."

Zeus caressed me, and called me his own. He covered my mouth again, lips caressing, tongue teasing, and I meandered on the periphery of euphoria until it grabbed me up and I was off and running straight into the fire again. His great hands went everywhere: fingers tangling in my hair, palms pressing my back, my sides, squeezing the curve of my behind. I loved the sensation of his touches, and decided then and there I might never get enough.

My own hands found his back, his chest, and between his legs an ample hardness that I felt almost unworthy of. Yet we were alone, just the two of us in his vast, soft bed. He strained for me. Only me. For the first time since my father sold me, I allowed myself to be flattered. I became more bold and ran my fingers up and down, and over the damp and swollen tip. He thrust into my grip.

We moved together in a slippery, graceful dance. Every time he touched between my legs, waves of heat washed over me. I could not hold back my moans. He rolled me to my back a second time and moved his kissing to my shoulders, chest and belly. He moved his head up and gave one command. "Lie still."

My fists gripped the coverlet and I pressed the back of my head into the pillows. A soft lapping began at the head of my penis. The impact of that stirred something very deep inside me as I cried out, shocked at how good it felt. As his mouth slowly engulfed me, the warmth and wetness on my sensitive skin filled me with joyous shivers. The purity of the moment could not even be contained in one word. I was happy but it was beyond mere happiness. It was aliveness and the ecstasy of that arrangement in my spirit.

When Zeus began to suckle, I cried out again. He held my hips down with both hands and moved up and down my length. I became displaced as a great throb overtook my entire body. I shouted when I came. It should not have been possible that the ecstasy went even higher as he continued to suck, but it did, and my organ throbbed many more times. The muscles of his tongue and throat pulled more and more from me as he swallowed.

I floated in reverie for a long time, thoughtless but full. Then, only a short time later, I wanted it again. His mouth on me, the sucking.

Zeus complied. He took care of me that night (if it could be called night, but it was hours and hours at the very least, in a room he made shadowed just for me) as no other ever had. I spent much of that time entering and exploring the realms of rapture, elated, burning, needful.

Zeus came, fiery, twice in my hand. I learned to love licking his cock as he had done for me, and the third time he came it was in my mouth with great spurts I could not manage to swallow, but that tasted like wine and made me even more amazed.

Since my eighteenth birthday, my life had become an existence of unfairness and despair. It seemed only just that I might find a place to forget myself for awhile, drunk on orgasms, a small but welcome reward.

I thought about the Lethe of the mind that Eros had mentioned. I almost understood the daily orgy parties Zeus threw. Almost. Though I knew Zeus had many lovers, I did not see the allure of more than one partner at a time. It seemed distracting. Less intimate. Unless avoidance of intimacy was the goal. But I wanted to feel wanted, and that I belonged somewhere. Zeus gave me that gift. First he'd given me Sable. And now this. It was through intimacy that I was finally able, for a little while, to receive the second.

13. Possessive Persuasion

From the beginning, thus far, as I lived with Zeus in his bed chamber, he never once tried to touch me until I'd given permission. After that, he still had not yet tried to penetrate me. I knew men did that. Even though I left during the orgy sessions in the throne room, usually to play games with Eros or to go back to Zeus's rooms to nap or read, I'd seen men doing it. I could not help but look even as I, a non-interested party, was escorted away.

The first time after our explosive intimacy that Zeus and I were back in the throne room, I sat on his throne as he conducted business through windows to other worlds. Mostly he stood to do this, or leaned against the armrest. Once in awhile he would reach out to caress my hair, or my naked shoulder.

Sable stood behind the throne, as always. Had he really moved to intervene the day I attacked Eros? I could not forget that. I constantly sought him out my peripheral vision.

I was exquisitely groomed today, dressed (if you could call it that) in a purple sash that covered me just enough to leave some things to the imagination. Sections of my hair were braided and woven into a gold, leaf crown. At the center of my chest lay a faceted emerald that, when it caught the light just right, flashed bubbles of green-prismed luminescence upon the walls. I had on a gold upper arm bracelet, many jeweled rings, and Zeus's prize servant Nomiki had oiled my skin to a bronze gleam.

I sat quietly, a book in my lap. Eros had taught me how to use a window to read but I still preferred the books I'd found in a library room I'd recently discovered. They were easier to handle than parchments and scrolls, and not as confusing as the crystal windows.

I had read nearly the entire book by the time Zeus clapped his hands and called for the usual chess game that preceded the orgies.

An uncomfortable knot tightened in my stomach. I glanced up quickly, closing my book. Zeus's black hair gleamed down his back, combed straight back from his face and affixed there with softly fragrant oils that made it shine. He wore his white linen skirt with a thick gold belt, the shortness of it showing off his powerful thighs. His wrists were bedecked with leather gauntlets inlaid with gold metal swirls. His chest and neck were bare, but on the crown of his head rested a circlet garland of green, fresh leaves with tiny white flowers that glowed against his black hair. Still, it was I who had gotten all the compliments.

The chess game was a silly display of errors as Zeus and Eros only half-heartedly competed, trading jokes back and forth in another language, jokes that I did not understand even when they were speaking Greek.

I had not spoken to Eros since I'd tackled him and he'd bested me on the floor in front of the throne. That had been days ago, right at the outset of my fever.

But now, as the chess game deteriorated, and people began to kiss and stroke each other, and those in chitons or robes stripped, the knot in my stomach twisted tight. Would they ask me to join in the group? Just the thought of it terrified me.

I glanced at Sable but ever since Zeus had taken me to his bed, Sable's eyes never met mine anymore. But sometimes, in the throes of ecstasy, I would see in a blink an image of his face, his eyes black and intent as if to ensure me he looked after me. Watched me.

I turned away from him.

All my attention focused on Zeus, the way light glistened in his dark eyes, the whiteness of his teeth as he laughed, the way his muscles flexed as he raised and lowered his hands, and walked up and down the lines of his chess pieces. No detail of him escaped me, which was why I also knew he was fully aroused under his skirt.

There were very few pieces in the game that weren't collapsed on the floor and beginning to embrace each other in ever-growing groups. Pawns rolled on top of bishops who in turn reached for rooks.

Eros made a move but Zeus was very distracted as two courtiers, one male, one female, came up behind him and began to stroke his back.

I got up from the throne and descended the marble steps. I came around the remains of the chess game and stopped in front of Zeus, looking up.

His eyebrows rose. "Ganymede? You surprise me." He took my hand.

"I do?"

"I did not think you would want to participate. At least not so soon."

Flames on my cheeks, I said, "I don't. I want you to come with me to your chamber."

Smiling, Zeus leaned down and kissed me firmly on the forehead, caressing my right arm, causing my body to tingle in arousal. "I promise I will be with you at the sleep cycle." Still smiling, he added, "Don't look so worried. My stamina knows no bounds." Then he leaned close and hugged me to him, whispering, "Ah, you are so gorgeous today. You make me feel wild again." He let go and winked at me. "Later for you, my love. But now I must also please my constituents and guests."

I opened my mouth to speak but nothing came out. Then I felt a hand clasp against my forearm and pull me away from Zeus. I turned, yanking back, only to see Eros, eyebrows narrowed, assessing me. He yanked back again and nearly dragged me to the balcony.

"Wait," I said behind gritted teeth. "Wait!"

But he did not wait. His strength was uncontestable, like the day he'd taken me to the floor, and he pulled me along as if I weighed less than a basket of his own blond feathers.

He led me to an ornate, cushioned bench that faced the balcony railing. "Sit!" he commanded me.

I looked back over my shoulder.

He pulled at my hand again. "Sit. Now! If you don't want to participate then that room is not for you right now."

Sable came out to the balcony with us and stood by the doorway, unruffled.

I glared at Eros, then sniffed once and sat. Eros remained standing, and leaned against the railing, his robe—today all of gold—trailing at his feet and billowing against his white wings in a whispery, gentle breeze.

"Why did you yank me so hard?" I complained, rubbing my arm.

"You were about to make a scene."

"I was not."

He tilted his head in admonishment.

I crossed my arms in front of my chest and looked down where the purple sash draped between my legs. Zeus's touch, and kiss to my forehead, had so immediately enflamed me, but now I was quite abruptly cool, limp.

"He is a very bad communicator," Eros said.

"What?" I kept looking down.

"Zeus does not explain things well. That is what he has mediators for. And councilors."

"Are you his councilor when it comes to me?"

When Eros did not immediately respond, I looked up. A half-smile quirked his lips. "Self-appointed."

"He didn't ask you?"

He shook his head. "Not that. But in the beginning he suggested I might teach you some things."

"Then why bother with me if it's not a command?"

"If you want the truth, at first I felt sorry for you, Ganymede."

I frowned. At the same time, tears threatened at the edges of my eyes.

He moved a little closer to me by the bench, but remained standing. "Don't be offended, little one. I've come to like you. Anyway, as I was saying, Zeus moves at the speed of—well—the speed of gods. He doesn't take his time to set the stage, so to speak."

I sat unmoving, silent.

"He doesn't feel any need to explain himself. Maybe he even forgets sometimes you're not from his world."

I didn't want to hear anything he had to say right now. "I want to go back to the chamber."

"Just let me say that Zeus has many lovers. All the time. And he might not feel a need to explain. Or even understand that you might be hurt by that—"

"I know he has other lovers!" I interrupted. And I did know, but not to my core. It was so easy for me to believe I was his only focus right now, even if only temporarily.

"Zeus is like the kind of man that wants to do everything at once."

I shrugged, my gaze burning straight into the clouds.

"It does not mean he doesn't love you."

"Stop talking!"

"Ganymede—"

"Just stop!"

Finally, Eros sat, not far, but not close. Tears threatened to spill from my eyes. But I did not want to wipe them away and bring attention to them. So I just sat. Fuming. What was wrong with me? Did I even love Zeus? I wanted him, but it was more a blissful habit than anything else. I'd grown used to his touches. Loved them.

I took a deep breath and looked upward.

As usual, the clouds had a quality of whiteness to them that was almost too bright to look at, but they were so tranquil, calming. The scents of the balcony wafted over us: locust blossom, orchid, bay.

After awhile, Eros spoke. "Have you thought more about wanting to learn to fight?"

"I'm trained in the sword."

"That's not what I meant."

"No. I have not thought more about it." I realized how curt I was being and didn't care.

"I like to be prepared for things, do research first, make plans, understand what might happen. But some things just don't work that way no matter how much you plan."

I had no idea what he was talking about so I just let his words wash over me, and remained unresponsive.

"Zeus is not like me. He is impulsive and does not plan for the long-term. Not usually. And so you were led here under the guise of mystery. I would have prepared you more. I would have—"

"Is that why you try to teach me? He never commanded you to. I never asked you to."

"It's what I do. I can be impulsive, too, but I like things to last. For awhile, at least."

"So if you don't agree with Zeus, why are you here at Olympus?" Now I brought my hand up and swiped it across my eyes. My body was still tense, but beginning to relax.

"I never said I didn't agree with him. He's ambitious, presumptuous and annoyingly uninhibited. He wasn't like that when I first met him."

"What was he like then?"

"Young."

102

A one word reply was not the story I was hoping for. I tried to imagine it though. Had Zeus ever been young?

Eros continued as if I hadn't interrupted. "He still has that passion from that bygone era, and that I can admire."

"That's it? Just because of that you stay here?"

"That." He paused, breathing deep. "And I love him."

Now I turned to look at him. "You?"

He smiled and I didn't like it. "We've been lovers off and on for centuries. One time we stayed married and faithful for sixty years. Another time, one hundred years."

"Zeus was faithful to you?" I could not imagine it. He was so sexually wild. "How old are you, then?" I remembered asking this question before and getting no answer.

"As I said before, I cannot, in truth, say it in a way you will understand. But I can say I have lived in Zeus's realm for nearly two thousand years."

Speechless, I could only stare at his green-gold eyes which glittered with far too much mirth for what he was saying.

Eros nodded at me, seeming to read my confusion. "It is very different here from your world. I know you haven't once forgotten that. But how different it is you are only just beginning to learn, sweetheart."

Two thousand years. My breathing sped up again. I turned my gaze back to the clouds.

"Let's relax, now, sweetheart. Cards or knucklebones?"

"Cards," I replied without really thinking.

By the time Eros finally escorted me back to Zeus's chamber for a nap, I had had many cups of wine to relax me, and we'd played at our games for countless hours. I was sated from the wine/ambrosia which always had an intoxicating effect. In addition, the wine surged through the body as if to pump the muscles and make the body feel virile and strong. I had seen perceptible muscle growth since I'd begun to drink the elixir, though my build remained slender.

Once I returned to Zeus's chamber, I headed straight for the bed, then turned when I saw the balcony doors were re-opened. The room was misted with saffron light. Sable, as always, had come with me, and stood by the balcony as if he'd never once moved from the moment I'd become ill until now.

I walked toward him, coming out onto the balcony and standing with my hand on the railing.

"You talked to me once," I said quietly. "I know you can again. But you won't, will you?"

No response. Of course, I did not expect one. But I couldn't help but remember the image of him that had come to me in the baths and at other moments of the pinnacle of ecstasy. It was as if he was right there with me in my mind, in my soul. All the time.

"I've been going through a lot and you've been there through it all. I want you to know I appreciate it."

I could still hear the tenor of his voice when we'd traveled away from Tros through the skies, through the stars. I realized now that Olympus was much further than just a sky away from Earth. I longed to hear him speak again if only in my mind.

I heard my words as if they came from far away.

"I really do appreciate it, Sable. And I'm asking you to stay even now that I belong to Zeus. I know I am just a foolish boy, but—" I looked up into his onyx eyes. The beautiful beak with the gentle upper curve glimmered. He held his tail feathers low so that they touched the floor. I could not see his arms, which were probably withdrawn into the thick and ruffled chest feathers. He looked made of midnight, my raven, but starless. Royal.

He was a shapeshifter who preferred this form, Zeus had told me. Found wounded in the depths of Void. That was all I knew. My voice a whisper, "I wonder about you all the time. I think about you."

The breeze ruffled his feathers. Then very subtly, he moved, a shift as if placing his weight more onto one foot. And I knew he would stay. For as long as I asked it of him.

14. Beauty in the Grove

I lay naked among the pinks of the sky-soft sheets, languid with wine, heavy with the pleasure of it. Everything still felt like bright shock, and now there was this new pleasure with Zeus where I rose up breaking again and again only to fall back in the liquid sun, the sweet aromas, the king's bed.

I watched Sable as I lounged on the pillows of Zeus's twilight-colored sheets, planning to nap the afternoon away. When the raven slept, he did so with one wing up, hiding an eye. He stood like that now; I wondered if he dreamed.

It seemed like hours before Zeus returned. I slept and had stunning dreams hazed over with pinks and browns as if I watched them happening through a window covered in autumn lace.

So much of what I dreamed would not fit into any description. But one dream stood out.

As often happens in dreams, you find yourself thrust into the middle of a story and you understand everything at the time but in the light of day that understanding fades.

In this dream, I lay hidden among branches and long-fingered leaves of a verdant bush. Shattered crystals of dew decorated everything about me, the plants, the honeyed blooms, the grass at my knees, even the air itself. Through the green-ness, I saw a fairy lagoon, azure as a stretched sky at noon. Fronds of pink and gold flora I could not name dipped their fragrance in the waters. A waterfall of slow-moving liquid trickled into the pool, amid the sounds of hidden insects purring, birds chirping. Rays of soft yellow light striped the scene.

The grass was velvet against my body, and I was content. The reason I stayed out of sight was because I was waiting. Watching.

When it appeared, my breath caught and held. My heart quickened.

A small raven flew down from above, landing on the beach of the lagoon. He hopped about for a moment, looking up, down, left, right. Then he bobbed his head all the way down until his beak touched the water. He moved his beak back and forth, swiping at the water, then lifted his head, drinking. When he finished drinking, he turned in a circle, not hopping now, but with a graceful swirl, one wing unfurling.

Three times he made that circle, turning and turning until a strange thing happened. His raven form began to grow. Both wings stretched outward now, and his neck elongated, his sharp-lined form softened to more graceful curves until I realized it was no longer a raven who stood there, but a black swan as elegant as a midnight hour. The swan sang and I heard words in my head.

"…sweet essence of the stars…the lush and tender soul…emits the everlasting beam of light…"

Though I did not understand the meaning, it was the most beautiful thing I'd ever heard.

The swan waded into the blue waters and swam, arching its long neck, seeming to feed on the fronds that bent to touch the pool's surface. After awhile of slow gliding along the surface, the swan, too, began to change.

I watched the head feathers grow long and sleek as the body itself morphed into flesh and muscle with arms, legs, chest, head. Now the form of a man stood thigh-deep in the water, olive skin glistening. His dark hair tufted at his neck and stuck up a little just above his forehead. He leaned his head back and spread his arms. Drops of water fell from them. He turned and I saw how strongly built his back was, where the wings had once been. His waist curved into narrow hips. He bent and caught water into his palms, then flung it up to the sky. When he turned again, I saw his face. The pink lips, the strong nose, the darkly arched brows. His high cheekbones gave him an almost gaunt appearance, but I knew he if smiled they would dimple and plump up. My eyes cast down his body. He was half-hard, brown shaft, pink tip, everything about him glossy, shining.

My fingers tugged at the grass before me, smooth and cool, and I imagined the grass was his hair and my hands were pushing it back, away from his face because I wanted to look at him, see him, draw nearer to him.

As he continued to fling water up and over himself at his bath, I stayed still as if in a timeless bubble, never wanting to look away, never wanting it to end.

But eventually, the glade grew shadowed. I opened my eyes in Zeus's bed, lying on my side, my hair damp with sweat at my temples, my breaths hard and fast. I clutched my fingers in the long fringe of a black pillow, then brought it closer to my chest and buried my face in its soft depths.

The pillow smelled of raven feathers, and flights through the stars.

Naked, aroused, I sat up blinking into the room's permanent light and sought the balcony entrance. There I saw him, head tucked under one wing, standing asleep.

Shapeshifter. Zeus had called him that. But even though he had arms that had held me, I'd never thought of him as a man shaped like me until now.

"Sable," I whispered into the air.

The raven's head and wing moved. He straightened. Then turned his head to look directly at me for the first time since my fever.

My mouth curved into a wide smile as I gazed at him.

Sable stood on the balcony in his tall man-sized raven form, expressionless as always, unmoving now except for a tender breeze that ruffled his feathers, exposing the iridescence of them: violet, bronze, royal blue. His presence comforted me, though my mind still remained silent of his voice. I so longed to hear it again. I kept having to convince myself that my memory of it was real and not yet another dream.

My body still yearned from the fading images of my dream. I looked right into his eyes and something inside me twisted in a warm, slow unfolding. I took a deep breath and held it.

There was grass under my knees again. Dew on the air. I felt myself starting to fall and startled with a jolt as the chamber doors opened and Zeus strode in.

My head jerked in his direction, but out the corner of my eye I saw Sable pivot away and return to his ever-fixed gaze on the clouds.

Zeus had his hands full, a goblet in each. Servants closed the doors behind him. His wide smile flashed upon me as he strode toward the bed.

"My boy, have you been napping all day?"

"I was with Eros most of the afternoon."

He stood over me, looking me up and down, stopping to stare at my arousal. "I see you are ready for me." He laughed and handed me the wine.

I drank thirstily. My blood heated. I thought of Zeus at the orgies, touching, caressing, fucking everyone but me. I was jealous and I knew it. Maybe that was why I'd had the dream. This feeling of incompleteness. Of wanting and wanting, never to be sated.

But no, that dream was special in a different way. I glanced at Sable, then drank more wine.

Zeus sat beside me, and reached out to run a hand over my thigh.

I set the goblet on the shelf over the bed. Then I leaned up, half sitting, my back against three pillows, and bent the leg he was touching at the knee. He ran his hand down, then up, up, and I bent my other knee and let myself fall open in

108

invitation. I didn't care anymore that the room was golden-lit. I didn't care that the balcony doors stayed open and Sable was just a few feet away. I wanted what I wanted. And that was sex with Zeus, hands on. I wanted everything in every way. I had waited all day.

Zeus ran his hand over my tight sac, caressing gently, pushing up with his palm. My erection tightened and bounced up.

Setting his wine aside, he drew himself up and into the bed, rolling onto his side and taking me into his arms. His hands smoothed down my back, cupping my buttocks, pulling me close. He kissed me with the noon heat of a Greek summer. My drowsy rapture from my dream became bright, vivid, immediate. I thrust against him.

He pushed me flat and licked his way down my chest, knowing I liked his mouth. Before, he had taken his time with me, but now he pressed his lips against my tip, tongue firm, and engulfed my penis in one, long downward motion. I held onto his shoulders, my fingernails digging into his skin, as he moved his mouth up and down.

I loved this act he'd taught me. But I wanted more. Thinking about the orgies again, I wanted it to be more.

"Wait," I whispered. He did not seem to hear me. "Wait." Louder.

Zeus lifted his head. "You don't want to come yet?"

I shook my head. "I want...I want you. Inside. Me." It was hard to say it. I took a quick breath when I'd finally gotten the words out.

I leaned back and pulled my legs up to my chest, exposing myself even more.

Zeus leaned over me, his erection trailing between my legs, swiping against the dampness he'd left on my own stiff flesh.

"You think you are ready for such things?"

I nodded, gazing at him with my eyebrows raised.

"You are more beautiful than words. I cannot resist you. You know that," Zeus said.

I smiled smugly. "I know."

He reached over my shoulder and brought out a jar. "The oils of Tirafian. They are exquisite for pleasure, keeping tenderness and pain at bay."

"Good." I took the jar from his hand and examined it. "It's what I want."

The little bottle looked carved entirely from emerald and was long and tapered in shape. I moved my fingers over it, only realizing some time later it was shaped like a penis with a soft cap at the end that popped off easily. I sniffed at the content. Spice and fire and earth came at me.

Zeus smiled at my expression. "The best."

I nodded. "I want it." I handed him the bottle, then turned over and onto my knees.

"Then you shall have it." His hand went to my buttocks, caressing, murmuring endearments and compliments. "My tongue first," he said. "To soften you."

My body tensed in excitement. My erection stretched forward, pointing at the head of the bed, and everything inside me wanted to burst free.

His hands spread me and immediately I felt the warmth of his tongue on me, right at the crack, teasing. It was almost too much. I couldn't keep myself from pushing back toward his mouth. He didn't seem to mind, nor did he stop what he was doing.

When I felt thoroughly soaked there, he sucked at my balls, then pulled my penis back and sucked the tip between my legs. His fingers moved over my puckered opening, slick and smooth. One entered. It did not hurt. I lost myself for awhile, only to realize there were two fingers inserted now, making ever-widening circles.

I pushed back and forth on those fingers until he took them away. Bereft, I glanced over my shoulder.

"I will go slowly," he said, meeting my eyes.

110

"I want you the way you fuck the people in your orgies. Like that." My words sounded crude to my ears but I didn't care.

He caressed my lower back, and ran his hands over my buttocks again.

"But you are so much more than that. You should be made love to. Every day."

But I wasn't thinking of love right then. I was thinking of how he had wanted them, the participants of his chess game, when he should have wanted me. I was thinking that even though Eros had said Zeus having many lovers did not mean he did not love me. But I wanted to be taken over by the sheer power of him, the way he was in the orgies. I wanted that Zeus. Because now I thought if he loved me too much, I thought I might cry. I just wanted to be fucked.

I felt more oil spread upon me. His hands opened me again. I felt the thickness of his cock probe, and I pushed back.

"Ganymede, wait!"

But I didn't want to wait.

He wrapped his arms around my waist and pulled me up to him, slowly, still not fully inside me, and began to caress my chest in slow-moving circles. "Slowly," he said into my ear. "Push out a little and you'll accept me better. Just feel me."

The pressure inside me was almost pain, but not. I pushed and felt as if I opened and took him deeper.

"Yes, that's it. It is too sweet, is it not?" he asked.

I rocked my hips to take more. My breaths came in gasps. "More!"

"Shhh." His hands moved over my stomach. His chest rubbed against my back. His push into me was agony and ecstasy, and took forever. I realized he was fully sheathed when his abdomen came up firm against my buttocks.

I rocked back.

His hands slid lower, grasping my cock and milking. I moved back and forth in his grip and realized his cock moved inside me in the same motion. It was utter bliss.

He left all the control up to me, and I went at my own pace, feeling it all, the emptying, the filling, that precious, firm heat. Hard flesh. And my insides slickly caressed.

It felt strange and wonderful at the same time. Impossibly full to a point of sickness that teetered into full-out pleasure. My entire body throbbed. His slippery hands squeezed and molded me, and there was a deep ache in my balls as he teased my sensitive flesh.

Suddenly, deep inside me, Zeus hit a spot that sent my mind careening. I cried out as a thundering pleasure rolled through me. The orgasm hit and I flew up straight out of my body until I was floating right where the tops of the walls opened to the sky.

Reeling in ecstasy, I saw myself crouched on the bed, knees bent, Zeus bent over me from behind, his magnificent body angled to hold me through it. His buttocks clenched, perfectly sculpted, and his hips thrust slowly, pushing the pleasure deeper. I realized I was watching myself being made love to.

The room had a misty, pink glow, like one of my dreams, the softness edged in a brilliant, lemon aura. Zeus's bed was like an Earth sunset, rumpled with red, pink and purple coverlets thrown back, and dark pillows strewn all over the bed and the floor. White walls rose up, columned on one side with great marble statues of horses, but clean and sparse the way Zeus like his palace. He told me he had actually borrowed the look, and the Greek language, from my own Grecian culture, and that he'd even lived in Greece as a child-god. "So you should feel very at home, boy," he'd said.

Through double doors, I saw the balcony overflowing with plants and flowers, ivy curling everywhere, the little dining table with its ornate, curving chairs. And Sable. His head was tucked under his wing, and one taloned foot was lifted close to the underside of his body as he slept in perfect balance.

But then I saw the glint of an open eye. He was not, in fact, sleeping at all. His head moved straight back and he looked directly at me. Not me on the bed, but spirit-me in the air. Floating. His black eyes watched me as I swayed on the air in my euphoria, reeling, flying, trembling in such a state of elation that I thought I could die right then and live in that state of grace forever.

Everything grew foggy in opal colors, but the blackness of Sable became more depthless as we stared at each other, a penetrating dark as if soon the stars would come out in him.

As I watched, part of that darkness separated and rose, still raven-shaped but ghostly now. Up he went, the essence of him moving faster, circling me until I spun to try to keep up with him.

All of a sudden he came at me and I felt a rush like cool rain with a burnt tang to it as he passed through my body, more than air, essence, heart, spirit. And then I was laughing. Falling. Streaming in the effervescent light, I re-entered my body piece by piece, Zeus still over me, Zeus embracing me and murmuring endearments.

Inside my mind, at long last, I heard Sable. For the first time since coming to Olympus, he spoke his silent, dulcet-toned language that only I could hear.

You haven't lived until you've burned like this.

I collapsed under Zeus on the silken bed. My face was wet, my golden hair tangled about my neck. I felt Zeus pull away, leaving me empty but damp, then turn in the bed and take me into his arms.

He kissed me, and then jerked his head up to look at me. "Not again. You are crying?"

I laughed. "No. I'm laughing."

He leaned forward, sniffing, then licked my cheek and nodded, almost grinning. "I see that you are not lying. Only tears of ecstasy are that sweet. It is a fine day when your first time in that manner can be so transforming."

"It is because I am with you." It was only a partial truth, for Sable had been there, too.

Zeus's arms closed around me, the side of my head pressing against his massive chest. I inhaled his fiery essence. Twined my legs with his. But I was not focused entirely on him. I peered over his bicep to the double doors where Sable stood, head tucked under one wing, a statue of a great bird, silent, unrevealed, ambiguous. A great mystery.

*

The hours melted in blue and gold along the hallways, balconies, libraries, galleries, the throne room. The days followed. Perhaps even months. I could not comprehend time here. I moved back and forth from lovemaking to the baths, my life comprised of pleasure, decadent richness, immortalizing wine, and sex.

Zeus was my only sexual partner, but when we made love there were those precious moments when Sable and I danced as if in a dream in the roofless space above the great bed chamber.

Zeus had many powers. He was a gifted man, an immortal man who called himself a god. But he did not see us dance. If he did see, he hid that knowledge from me very well.

I enjoyed Zeus. Maybe I even grew to love him, in a way. But I grew to love the airy dance more, and anticipated it every day, looking forward to that moment more than anything else.

Because Zeus had so many sexual partners, I did not feel I was betraying him by sharing my ecstasy with Sable. But the instinct within me to keep Sable and his mental abilities a secret remained strong. I said nothing about it. Not to Zeus. Not to Eros. They had told me only about his shapeshifting, and merely the name of his species. Solumnist. No one offered more information. No one even seemed to think it relevant.

I kept quiet about my reverence for Sable.

15. Be the Cosmos

Summer at Olympus stretched eternal. It kept everything flaxen and glossy, tasting of syrup, scented with honey, milk, rose. Time did strange flips. Millennia might pass by, Eros once told me, and one would not notice.

Eros never treated me differently after my fever, other than that day when he'd dragged me from the orgy in the throne room, and even then he'd been calm, and kind. He did not comment much upon my activities behind closed doors with Zeus. He never again offered to teach me to fight, although I think Zeus would have liked to see it, my lesson played out in physical sweat and strain, me and Eros wrestling naked in front of the throne.

Nearly daily, he took me to the balcony and taught me more games. Strange card games which I quickly caught onto. Like poker, which was great fun. I taught him draughts and backgammon. Chess, though, was always played in the throne room with live people as the pieces.

I figured out that Eros was not really interested in games. He used the meditative distraction of some of the slower ones to talk. His talk was never about wine or the daylight or regular palace gossip. He thought deeply. He spoke deeply. He went slowly, at first, for my benefit, but after awhile I realized he was succeeding in his teaching of me.

He made little comments that forced return questions from me.

Sun-bathed, holding what I decided had to be a winning Rummy hand, I asked. "What is it to be immortal?"

He did not look up from his cards. "You heal from wounds. You don't get sick. You don't die."

"I know all that. I mean what is it like...how is it? A life of...of...forever?"

He grew thoughtful, his eyes greener with the enticement of what could only be intellectual stimulation, although I was far off from being any sort of intellectual equal with him. "First let's look at mortality. When one is mortal, one is created by the past, we are its skeleton with modifications, we are its clouds, its sunsets, its sleeping passion shaped by personal events that snag us into their business, make us dependent. Left to our immortal soul's devising, we would dance in the rain forever but our sensitivity to cold sends us indoors, along with our fear of sickness, death. Events are cellular."

"I don't understand 'cellular'."

"We are made up of millions of cells in our bodies, each one a rift through which we walk, these doorways to ourselves, often hidden, locked, and the keys are made of wonder and terror and tears, golden days and onyx nights, snow, wind, stars..." He could go on like that for long moments, sometimes entire games of chance.

"What does this cellular thing have to do with immortality, then?" I asked, trying to steer him back to territory I could comprehend.

"Immortality opens those locked-door cells, gives every opportunity for every cell a chance to live and keep living, trying every way until you hit a wall, then finding an opening in that wall and moving on to more. It imbues every part of you with your soul, pouring through you never stopping. Every possibility, every thought you think could come into being. There is time enough. You have long enough. You will not stop. It is the universe ever evolving."

I gave a heavy sigh, set down my hand. "Gin," I said, smiling up through my lashes.

He fluttered his wings, looking slightly annoyed. "Do you understand any of what I was saying?"

I shrugged. "I understand I beat you five games in a row."

"And that is one possibility we have now explored. But there will be infinite variations, if we so choose those directions, to have marathon games where I will win a hundred or a thousand times in a row, or you will, or we will both throw the cards away and invent our own games we have yet to imagine."

"Boredom."

"What?"

"Immortality sounds like it consists largely of boredom."

"It is a choice immortals make for themselves."

I bristled at the word 'choice'. "I never had a choice. I came here as if in chains."

"Your father and Zeus are kings. Kings come with their own brands of morals."

"Trouble."

Eros frowned. "You are full of one word phrases today."

I leaned on my upturned palm as Eros dealt from the freshly shuffled deck. "Leaders are trouble."

"Leaders get things done when no one else can."

"They hurt."

"They move a species forward. Or sometimes backward. But even the back-steps are a way of moving as time seeks to make sense out of chaos."

I picked up my cards, trying to focus on them, but I could not see. I had made love with Zeus. I did not want to think of anything but that pleasure. And yet what he had done by taking me, purchasing me, never ever left my mind.

Eros discarded. "You say you have no choice. But you will learn—or maybe you never will—that everything must come out of you, be you, and be in you. You are whole, but you just don't know it. You are reality and reality's creator. You must create everything, both dissolution and decay, that which is transient and fugitive, treacherous and faithless. But also that which is boundless, perpetual, and enduring maybe even only in a thought or a deed. Self-sufficiency. Self-reliance. Something from nothing. Nothing from everything. These things will come from you and they will be unique and beautiful and yours. The only things you cannot create are replacements, in exact duplicate, of the two main building blocks of creation. Life, which is chaos itself trying to find form. And love. They are your primary ingredients, founded before the universe was born."

"Not hate and death?"

Eros shook his head. "Merely sub-categories. Your turn."

"Babies are created, then born."

Eros shook his head. "They are new life, yes, but not exact duplicates of the parents. I want to be specific. Life is created, but it cannot be repeated. Not in the exact same way. There will always be a variation. Thus, everything," he emphasized, "everything is precious."

"Evil is precious?"

"Evil is perpetrated, interpreted. It is a wrong deed according to a constructed law of perception, different depending upon context. But not a thing unto itself. It is not a real force. Life is a force. Love is a force."

"Life and love is all. You keep saying it. I heard you. DNA." I did not ask it as a question and realized I probably sounded a bit peeved.

"That is it. You are the cosmos unto yourself."

But right now I did not feel like it. Eros had dealt me a terrible hand.

And so they went like that, our conversations, day after day. I could not help but slowly absorb what he said, until I realized I was thinking and talking like him, sometimes to anyone who might listen including Sable, and the motionless statues in the baths.

16. Of the Wine Immortal

I learned more about the alien properties of Olympus through the endless days.

There were no dark spaces. Even closed rooms emitted light. Everything was illuminated, intoxicated, and carefree. My tears had long dried.

But once in awhile I heard the air keen the wind's deep grief. It reminded me I would never go home.

The wine gave me a precious feeling, a surge of potency, a sense of dominion. But over nothing. For I owned nothing. I was nothing.

But in Zeus's arms, and with Sable and our dance, I found my passion. Something wakened in me I'd never known before. When Zeus called out, "Ganymede," I always went to him and stood by his side, or stretched out in his bed waiting. Zeus had taken me from my home. Now I was taken again and again to furious, burning heights from a simple caress of his hand. He was my field and my firmament. I became infinite in him. And with Sable in our astral dance.

And yet that boundlessness reached out to an emptiness that still needed to be filled. I reached out more often to Sable.

The one sentence he'd uttered that first time we danced never left my mind: *You haven't lived until you've burned like this.*

Since then, we flew together in my ecstasies, and he always rushed into me at the end, but in those moments he had returned to his usual silence. No more pretty words or thoughtful remarks.

I wondered why. Sometimes he seemed to nod at me, or tilt his head. But why he was so still, so isolated and contained, I longed to know.

When we were alone, often I would go to the balcony to sit. Sometimes I'd talk to him about my home, or about my conversations with Eros, which I suspected he had already overheard since he followed me everywhere. I thought about immortality and what I did not confess to Eros, I told to Sable.

I wasn't always sure if he heard me. He did so little but stand or raise one wing and sleep. Sometimes I caught him watching me, sometimes he faced the clouds in another direction. He always followed me to the baths and to the throne room. But he never gave any indication he was actually participating in anything with me until we danced. And even that, while I knew it was real, was a part of him escaped from the solid being he was, the one who had held me all the way from Earth to Olympus, who had kept me safe during that journey encased in his arms, his feathers, his protective self. I realized as a shapeshifter he had shifted into something that had held me in my sleep in a sort of timeless stasis where I could not be harmed, so that the journey itself never stressed me in any way.

That, alone, was an amazing fact about him. In my dream he'd become a swan and then a man. But who was it really that I danced with in my moments of ecstasy? What was he?

On a particularly bright day, when everyone seemed in a good mood and Zeus's work had gone well, I went off with Eros after the live chess game, and he sat me in front of a floating screen that appeared in mid-air and taught me some games I'd been resistant to for so long. I had learned—very badly—to use the smaller devices that fit in the hand for reading, but not much more.

Some magic windows, I learned, saw only games through their frame, or books, music and artwork. Others were gateways to many worlds.

Now, very patiently, and using games to help teach, he showed me how to better navigate the mystery of that magic. I could use controls to watch living people doing things.

"Are these like plays?" I asked.

"Some of them are stories for entertainment, and some of them are real scenes from things that are happening far far away."

I pondered that for awhile, shifting on the pillows, learning how to use my hands to gesture for changes of scenes, or steady my voice to command new subjects.

Eros said, "People on the 900 worlds speak many, many different languages. But your screen is programmed to present it to you all in Greek."

"That's—that's—how does it do that?"

He smiled. "For you it is new. For us, here, it is old. But it is quite a feat of technology."

"So anything is on here for the asking?"

"Some things may not be. But you can find out why they are not, and perhaps where to look for them elsewhere."

"So, like Zeus, I could bring up the image of Tianzun and talk to him?"

"Yes, but he is a very busy man and might not be available. You would be put into a queue to speak to him eventually. Or perhaps he would ignore you altogether."

I frowned. "He seemed nice, though. He acknowledged me."

"Ah, well, you are a hard one to ignore." Eros patted the top of my head.

"So all of wisdom might be found within this magic?"

"All?" Eros raised one eyebrow. "I would not say so. You cannot experience life for yourself within these windows. Not beyond a certain level. You might learn a great many things, wisdom included, but I am of the belief that wisdom is no replacement for the force of life itself."

"In my world, some hierophants say that when one is enlightened with wisdom, they may transcend life."

"Hmm. I would say—" Eros put a hand to his beardless chin. "No."

"No?"

"Wisdom can be used for many things. It might help prevent tragedy, illness, or great destruction. It can make life better because with it you are armed with information to steer through the obstacles that fall onto your path. But just because you might gain this knowledge, attain what you call enlightenment, then that is the moment you would give up life? Why?"

"Go to a higher realm, I suppose."

"And where would that exist?"

"I don't know. Beyond death."

"Ah, but you did not say your hierophants would die. You said they would transcend life."

"Is that not the same?"

"Is that what you believe?"

He kept answering my questions with questions. I knew why he did it. He was teaching me to think for myself. Helping me gain my own wisdom through other means than reading it through a window.

I said, "If death is the end, and there is no Underworld, or Elysian Fields, no spirit world or River Styx, then those who transcend life and don't die would exist maybe separate from the dead in another time and place. But I am not sure death is an end. I am not sure the transcendence of life and death isn't the same."

Eros watched me carefully. Softly, he said, "Where do you think you are now?"

I looked around me from our table to the flowering plants in pots and the orange tree where Sable stood, and over the railing at the clouds so white they seemed to shimmer with a pure and absolute reality. "I certainly don't feel dead."

"Good." He laughed, and I loved the tone of him in that moment. "That's a relief."

"But none of you ever die? Ever?"

122

He picked up his goblet and drank. "This wine," he said, setting the cup down. "Is like wisdom. It offers transcendence. An everlasting effect of that, so to speak. What it does not offer is life. That is what we ourselves do. That is what we decide. What we create."

I wanted to say I didn't get to make decisions. I had been brought here with no occasion to choose. Instead, I said, "So like the magic window, the wine is not life itself. We are."

"You are quick, Ganymede. It is refreshing to see it in one so young and from such a superstitious and barbaric world."

I almost felt offended. But I realized he was not wrong. I had never believed in the gods, not as they were defined by the word "god" to be precise. But my world was superstitious about it. And about centaurs in the wood, and unicorns and fairies. However, didn't the existence of Zeus himself, and Olympus prove me wrong? Wasn't I taken by a magical bird? And wasn't it Sable who'd told me in my mind that my grandmother had been a nymph? Were these people secretly visiting mine and having relationships? Certainly, it seemed so. Zeus had come for me, after all. But I still did not believe it was the least bit supernatural, even if the only word I had to call their "technology" had been magic. I refused to believe it on the level of "divine" where I had to worship it forever and be its cup-bearer.

For long moments I sat there, my mind whirling with questions, realizations, powerful thoughts. And for a fleeting instant I had it. The way out. The briefest sensation that I wasn't trapped, that there was a way back. I simply did not have all the information I needed yet.

I held the thin window, which was about the size of my head, slightly up.

"Does this window see everywhere?"

"As I said, some are limited. Some see many things."

"I know. You told me it depends on how I do the looking." I took a deep breath. "Could this one see Earth?"

"Surveillance of Earth is private. For now."

I shook my head. "I don't understand."

"It means no, not just any window can see Earth."

"But some can."

"Yes."

"Which ones?"

Eros glanced away. I thought I saw Sable sway for just a moment.

"As I said, that is a private matter."

"Private. But how? To some people? To one person? Zeus found me. Can it be seen only through his window?"

"Think of it like this. If you have a room and you only invite certain people into it, only those people will ever see it. If you open that room to allow anyone who wants to pass through it, that is public."

My mouth hardened. "I know the difference between public and private!"

"Earth is a room that is private. And that is all I will say on the matter."

I slammed the window a little hard on the table. It bounced once, unharmed. I stood, kicking the pillows aside, and looked out over the balcony. Down as far as I could see were more clouds and more blue sky. Nothing else. I saw no land, no other palaces in the clouds. Nothing.

In my lungs, the air burned and trembled. I realized my hands were fists. I heard shouts and laughter from indoors. Everyone having fun with their ostentatious decadence, a chess game of an orgy. Nothing wrong with that. People seeking pleasure. People enjoying themselves. Certainly I had learned this way of release and relaxation. It was how the body worked in life and love if one enjoyed that sort of thing. And I did delight in it, but not in the way that Zeus did. Not with strangers. Not with people looking at me, analyzing me, admiring me but only in the way they defined that admiration. No one saw the true me and I was too self-conscious to see any freedom in that. As if I both wanted and hated being the center of attention. As if I could not decide.

Behind me, Eros finally spoke. "You need to learn who you are. That is not accomplished by going back, only by going forward."

"You're being cryptic. I don't see what's so wrong with wanting to see Cinth again. Or Pal."

"What if they did not recognize you?"

"I haven't changed." Had I?

"What if you had a greater destiny and they held you back from that?"

"I don't believe in destiny." Tears rolled down my face. I hadn't noticed until I felt them drip onto my hands where my fingers clutched the railing.

"Nor do I," Eros said.

"But something in my DNA, something you said about it made Zeus take me." My voice sounded damp and muffled.

"He is attracted to those who might survive. He is a creator, after all."

"Survive what? Creator of what?"

"He is a molder, a maker, an artist. His immortal kingdom is reliant, for longevity, on new blood. But only those who are made for the ages can even be considered. You are not someone who sees and thinks in simple ways, in black and white absolutes. But it is more than that. Your DNA structure predisposes you as having the gift for longevity. To survive the ages."

"If it's in my blood, then it's in my sister's blood, too. And my brothers."

"Not always." I didn't see him shrug, but I felt it on the air. "And, as I have also said before: Zeus is impulsive. He saw you. Not them."

I was trapped in a curse, my beauty, my youth. My DNA. Helpless, I did not have a say in any one decision.

"You are feeling helpless right know. I know."

"Not helpless. Tethered. Caged. And you are the jailer."

"The jailer who will set you free."

I turned, scraping my hand back through my rumpled hair. "When?" My voice shook. "After they've all gone to dust, my family, my home, the origin of my birth?"

"How long do you think you've been here already?"

I shrugged.

"It is not the same here, the way time moves. But Zeus has found a way to record it all, and send images where he wishes in the same continuum. He negotiated with your father from a far off vantage using an image of an old, wise man. But he can use any image he wants."

"Is he a shapeshifter like Sable?"

"Not like Sable. Though when one becomes as old as we, the mind learns to assign whatever image it desires to the body, hair color, eye color, etc. But actual, organic shapeshifting is a rare talent, unequivocal to all else. When Sable brought you here, he shifted into a lightship complete with stasis field and stardrive. Only a few life forms in the known galaxy can accomplish such a feat. Even the oldest of us still use technology for that sort thing."

Sable shifted into a ship? I had never thought of it that way. Why was Eros telling me? I always knew Sable could be a conveyance. Sable could be an escape. But then there was the question of Sable. He did not speak. Only twice had his lovely voice breached my mind. Where did his loyalties lie? With Zeus, of course. He had been with Zeus from the beginning, sitting on the shoulder of an old man in my father's court, and then taking me at Zeus's command. Sable had brought me here. He had never, ever indicated that he'd be willing to return me. He followed me around because I'd asked for him and Zeus had commanded it. We danced in ecstasy, yes, but Sable had never implied fealty to anyone but Zeus.

Somewhere deep, I felt a crucial pain at that thought.

Eros motioned with his hand, decorated with gold rings. "Sit back down, boy." He set aside his window. "We've spent hours with the windows. Let's play some cards."

I wiped my face on the back of my hand and stared down at him.

"Come on," he said. "Relax a little. I will have more wine brought. And chocolate."

I had never had chocolate until Olympus. Such a delicacy. My mouth watered. Eros tempted me. Zeus tempted me. And then there was Sable and the dancing rush. It was hopeless.

"For now," I said, not smiling. I flopped back onto the pillows as Eros put my window away and began to deal the cards.

Still, I could not expunge the thought that Earth, my own home, was Zeus's private room to which I apparently needed an invitation. I knew Zeus would never give it. So that left me one remaining option. I would have to take it.

17. In the Purple Hours

I waited for Zeus. I dreamed.

High over the world I went. Everything in a golden decay. Earth was a fairy tale. Olympus was a myth. Steady. Steady. I flew. Slow storms formed around me. Then I spun among fast stars and moons. And I, within it all, the center.

I was not moving. I was moving. Time brooked by like purple streaks in sunset skies.

Briskly leaping wind. Sky hunched in grief. Clouds. And through them the columns of Olympus poked, as if in resentment toward anything not as pristine and perfect as its hazel days, its nightless nights, its walls brimming over with ecstatic force.

It had been so long ago now since I first circled that white monstrosity. An alien bird with a conglomerate gene pool residing inside me. And even longer that I had wandered the stars in search of the shroud of Lethe, that drape of soft forgetfulness that calmed and healed and renewed. It was a velvet abyss, and I lay within it a wounded creature, and slowly allowed the healing of forgetfulness take me.

When Zeus called to me, I woke as if from a dream of a thousand years. I perched on his shoulder in all my glory, touched the sun of him, the splendor. It was not difficult to love him, to be his messenger, his mode of conveyance from Olympus to Earth, where I learned to love the raven. To be the raven.

I picked the raven to stay inside me because he was black-winged. Defiant. The ultimate pilot of its own mind.

As reward for my service and love, Zeus gave me my own aerie in the clouds, away from the noise and chaos of Olympus. He knew I appreciated it. He knew I would always be there when he called.

I woke amazed, for the dream was not mine and I knew it. I sat up and felt, for the first time, a frisson of cold. The light in the chamber looked dimmer for a change, old, until I realized Sable stood in the doorway of the balcony shadowing the light from that direction. Overhead, the blue sky went on in its endless exhale.

Sable was usually outside the room. But now he was inside, and had obviously been watching me sleep. I got up and went to stand in front of him, looking him in the eye. He did not flinch.

I said, "You sent me a sad and beautiful dream."
Nothing.
"Like with the dancing." I nodded upward to let him know I meant the way we came out of our bodies and went into the air. "Only dreaming."
No response.
"I had another dream of you awhile back. You were a swan swimming in a pool, and then a man."
I was used to him not moving, staying silent in my mind. So I moved about the room, rummaging, still talking. I

wanted him to know I acknowledged his presence, and that I also liked it.

I opened a closet with robes and chitons and leather skirts, and went through it, then moved on to a drawer of gauntlets. More drawers of jewelry, gold, silver, precious gems. The shelves over the bed held a few real books, a chest of containers of assorted oils, my book from Cinth, my reading window, and jade, onyx and marble sculptures of centaurs, horses with wings, beautiful people half-draped, half-naked in poses of yearning, longing and thoughtfulness. Zeus had an obsidian cube that was hot to the touch. But I found none of his personal windows.

On the wall by the door was a window I had been shown by the servants when I'd first arrived. That one functioned to call them. It also had an ability to show me moving pictures of rooms around the palace as well, but that seemed to be the extent of its function. I never used it.

But today I went to it and called upon my memory of some of the teachings from Eros to fiddle with the controls.

I saw my favorite library and gallery where a few people wandered about or read. I saw one of the bigger balconies filled with partiers dancing, playing music and fucking. There were long halls lined with private rooms for sleeping. The window did not see all the way into those. On my last tap, the window brought into focus the throne room. Beside the throne, Zeus lay on a padded bench getting a massage. Eros stood beside him. They were talking but the window was silent.

I looked for a volume switch and much to my surprise I found one. Their voices came up and I could hear them speaking earnestly. Unfortunately, it was not Greek they spoke. I had picked up some words and phrases of their strangely hushed language. Like a lullaby, they spoke, lilting and drawn out, pretty like harp-tones. I tried to remember what Eros had taught me about adjustments for the windows. I looked for a language adjustment setting. But there was nothing that helped me. Finally, I just addressed the window itself with my voice. "Speak Greek."

Suddenly I could understand them. But they still talked of things I didn't have a context for, names of people and places I did not know. I wandered about the room some more, snooping, finding nothing. Then I heard my name.

I looked back at the window on the wall.

Eros stood with his wings half-unfurled, a blond-white background to his darker amber-robed form. "Ganymede wants access to Earth."

"Earth is locked down at the moment," said Zeus.

"But you've left people behind."

"They wanted to stay. The mix of other races with humans is good for their system. It produced Ganymede, did it not?"

"Yes."

"And he is lovely."

"And terribly homesick," Eros replied.

"He's settling in. Certainly, he seems to have no complaints in bed."

My cheeks heated to hear this.

Eros sighed. "No one has complaints from you in bed."

Zeus laughed. "Are you flirting with me now?"

"I'm the god of love. I'm flirting with you all the time, aren't I?"

Laughter.

"I'm just warning you to keep your private windows away and hidden," Zeus said. "I don't think it would be good for him to look back right now. He's still learning and adapting. The ambrosia has taken a good, strong hold on him, but if he is pulled in to human mortal ties so soon he might lapse, or suffer a break in the mind."

I tried to stay calm as I listened. Sable did not move, but instinctively I could feel his tension.

Then, as quickly as they had been talking, with ease and humor, they both went silent. Eros shuffled his wings back and forth, then walked away without another word.

All Zeus said was a command to his masseuse. "The left shoulder. Deeper."

A low hum sounded. The usual noise of the throne room had quieted. It was still bright and sunny, but the sleep cycle had come on, and people were retiring to their rooms.

I looked at Sable. At that moment, he turned from me until his back was to the room again, and he faced the white-clouded sky. I felt instinctively rebuffed. Suddenly paranoid. Had he communicated some message silently to their minds for my sake?

I realized there was no one in Olympus I knew whom I could really trust. There never had been.

18. Looking Back

I was reclining in bed and reading aloud, thinking Sable might appreciate it, when Zeus returned to the chamber. Despite my suspicion that Sable had notified Zeus of my espionage, I still felt the most trust of anyone in Olympus for the big raven. It was because of his original promise to me. *I will protect you. I swear it.* His calm voice still whispered those words in an echo of my memory.

Zeus took no notice of Sable, who had hours ago moved back into the room from the balcony as I read. Zeus came straight to me, undoing his short skirt as he walked, dropping it to the floor. His skin gleamed from the massage oils. He was half-hard, although it was such an ordinary state that taking notice of it seemed as uninteresting as taking note he was breathing. Zeus was always aroused. It was the ambrosia in the wine. Its vibrancy in our systems made the body zing with life, potency, the blood always churning even when the body was at rest.

He sat on the bed beside me, raised his arms over his head and pulled the pillow up to cushion his back as he leaned against the headboard. His dark hair hung loose and shining against his jaw-line. Muscles rippled in his stomach and along his ribs. His legs shone in perfect sculpted beauty. His dark cock angled to one side, resting for the moment. It was difficult to look away from his entire magnificence.

I put down the book and Zeus idly picked it up, looking at the binding. "Do you find my library of Greek literature to your tastes?"

"You have books I've never seen or heard of."

"That is a 'yes' then?"

I nodded. Out the corner of my eye, I saw Sable retire to the balcony and tuck his head under his blue-black wing. But I guessed he would not be sleeping. Not for awhile at least, until after Zeus and I had sex.

Zeus looked up and down my body, half-covered with pillows in my laziness, and began to slowly push them away. Eyebrows arched, he asked, "Have you been waiting for me?"

"Of course." A flip in my stomach. A two-fold apprehension. First, because I worried that he knew of my window-observation of the throne room. Second, because I could not resist my sensual longing for him.

As he pushed one pillow away from my abdomen, he let his thumb trail along the tight skin just below my navel and surges of pleasure shot through my groin. My nipples hardened, as well as my penis, which had been somewhat sedate up to that point.

Zeus drew his hand up my tummy to my chest, neck, chin, lifting my face up toward him and placed a slow, warm kiss to my lips. His fingers moved from there to my hair, gently combing.

This man had taken me. This man was keeping me from my home. This man who was not a man but something else had caused me untold upheaval. I hated him. I wanted him. And in a way, I loved him.

I lifted up, one bent knee falling back against a velvet pillow, my hands rising to clasp his broad shoulders. He was slippery, smooth, hard.

I opened my mouth under his and became lost.

He pressed both his hands into my hair, pulled me up and ran them down my back. His hands went lower and urged my hips to meet his. I spread my legs and straddled him as he rolled onto his back, still sitting partially up against the pillow. I leaned over him, rubbing my backside over his thighs, then up to encounter the hardness between his legs. I moved my buttocks back and forth over it as he held my hips tightly. He pulled back from my face to whisper my name, then kissed me harder and with such passion I was filled up with his dark light.

Having Zeus as a lover: no complaints. He always took his time. He was tender and considerate. He never criticized me, or asked me to perform some sexual deed. He waited for me to ask, or to offer. It was his way in bed. In the outside world, with his windows to business and war, he could be analytical and severe. I'd often heard him argue in his commanding tone, or rant to places I could not see in the windows. But it did not work that way for him in bed. Even what little I saw of his orgies had him only accepting offers and engaged in offering himself. His choreography of the piles of sexual bliss was less commanding, more a game.

The commands I received from Zeus in life outside of bed were more along the nature of "sit here", "stand there", "drink this", "stop crying."

Tonight, he held me against him as I sat in his lap. He ran his hands all over me with a reverence that let me know I was wanted. Back home I had had what I would call suitors from both genders, but I ignored them. They were noble young people my own age who did not interest me. But this powerful man who wanted me and made me want him back spun my head, destroyed my childhood walls.

I wanted to be encompassed by him, and encompass him. I let him lay my body back in the bed and explore. I opened myself to him fully. He left roses on my neck, and suckled my nipples to hard nubs. His wet tongue laved the insides of my thighs and delved into the crease of my buttocks as he lifted my hips in his powerful grip and tongued his way up from my entrance to my balls. He lavished sweet attention on them as well, before licking up my cock and sucking at the tip. I could not keep still. My body undulated at such intrinsic pleasures, his gift to me. I reeled in amazement, a natural light-headedness.

His supreme patience nearly drove me mad. Long after I was ready, and his teasing kept me in a state of tense desire, he finally turned me onto my stomach. Had his way.

I sobbed when he entered me. My body was predisposed to receive him. Molded, sculpted and arranged so perfectly that we fit together as if we'd always been doing this, had never been apart. Deep inside, a part of me resented the fact that sensually we were in such impeccable harmony. I resented it because something was left behind. In this way we were matched, and I was comforted, and I loved sleeping in his arms, but I was missing a part of it. I was sure of this. Otherwise, why did I feel so good and so lonely at the same time?

Even in his arms, riding to ecstasy, I was homesick. But this extra feeling of emptiness was more than that.

How warm he was. How explosive. I could only respond in kind, pushing back, craving to be closer to him, desiring more. I wanted my loneliness to vanish. I wanted to feel complete.

Maybe after everything, I asked too much of myself. Or maybe no one ever felt that connection all the way with anyone and we were beings meant to be apart from final communion.

Or maybe I was just too young.

He stroked that special place inside me with his wonderful rhythm and I was off, splitting open, pulsing, coming, flying straight up to the sky. To freedom. To my raven.

We floated toward each other, slowly revolving just beyond the heights of the chamber. The pink fog shrouded us in a private circle of light apart from everything, just the two of us floating, leaping gracefully around each other as we had done so many times before. But this time, when Sable rushed toward me and we mingled, I didn't fall straight back into my body. We hung together, still aloft, joined together in every cell, and I heard my mind shout for joy as if into an abyss. I twirled with him in a timeless void, enmeshed in his soft black down. And for that moment my loneliness, my homesickness, lay abandoned in another space.

It was only then that my ecstasy rose even higher, beyond description.

I saw my body writhing on the bed. It was nothing compared to this immaterial state, this all encompassing sharing with Sable.

When I finally re-entered my body, Zeus was holding me in his arms, softly calling my name. He had come inside me. I could feel it, but I didn't remember it. He turned me to face him, smiling.

"There you are," he said. "That was unlike all the times before. You fainted, I think."

I smiled up at him. "Beyond the apex of the pleasure, I just kept going up and up." It wasn't entirely a lie.

"Ganymede, you are so special. I want to give you everything. Anything you like."

I looked at the raven on the balcony, head tucked, perhaps truly asleep now. Perhaps not.

Then I gazed up at Zeus's brimming dark eyes.

"What would you like?" he asked.

A pause. A moment. My will forming into a demand.

"A window to Earth."

Though he held me close, the immediate tension in our bodies at my request felt as if it was trying to wrest us apart. Very quietly, our damp bodies still embraced, he said, "I am aware you wish this. But I also know now is not the right time for you to have that. For your own well-being, the ties must be firmly cut."

"No. I don't accept your statement." Did anyone ever speak to Zeus like this? I felt both ashamed and bold. I stared at his chest rising, falling. If I had been at new heights only a short time ago, now my body sank to the furthest of lows. I closed my eyes. At my core came a fluttering, a tremble. Why was I surprised? I knew the answer would be 'no'. Eros had already told me that I couldn't go back. That it would not be allowed.

"My sweet boy," Zeus said. "I want everything for you. Everything. I do not want you to feel this pain. But right now, the interference of your past cannot be. You must trust me on this matter."

Trust? For the man who had abducted me? My mind warred between anger and confusion and outrage. My father had sold me to a stranger from a star no bigger than a grain of sand in Greece's night sky. Zeus had bought me for a fortune. I was in a nightmare of horror and pleasure, dream and dread, and could not wake.

Not knowing how to react, my mind shut down. I lay limp and unmoving in Zeus's arms. My eyes stayed closed. He settled me against his side, pulling the pillows around me to cushion me, draping a sheer coverlet, gentle as air, over my body, tucking me in as if I were a child.

"I do not want you to be so sad," Zeus whispered.

I lay unresponsive. Closed.

"You do not yet begin to know how special you are, *paidi mou*."

I had never heard him use that Greek endearment before. It meant, literally, 'child', but in my culture, it was meant for anyone, and with much more affection than that simple word.

I hated him. But I couldn't hate him. A small sound of pain escaped my lips.

Zeus's fingers caressed my cheek, back and forth. I tried to keep my breathing shallow, but it only served to make it more erratic.

Finally, he said, "Would it help you if I told you your family is well? They are happy. They are healthy. They are wealthy."

I opened my eyes. He lay very close to me, but taking care not to crowd. "They don't miss me?"

"Of course they do. But life marches on. They have their lives to seek and follow as you do yours."

"But Cinth? Is she well?"

"Of course. I would not allow it to be otherwise."

"But I need to see. I want—"

"I know. She was your favorite, yes?"

I nodded, swallowing deeply. "Her book is on the shelf. The one she made for me."

"Ah, the pretty poetry written out in such a beautiful hand." He glanced up where I had stored Cinth's naming day present to me. "A very special gift."

"She's special." I swallowed again. "Zeus, could you send Sable to bring her here?"

His brows narrowed as if slightly pained. "Enough," he said. "I've told you enough."

"But why not?"

"Because not everyone is made for the ages. You are immortal now. Most cannot endure it. You have the ability inside you, and so time will test you and see if it is so."

"But Cinth has my mother's blood in her, too!"

"It is not the same, Ganymede. I'm sorry."

"Then I don't want it!" I sat up fast, nearly striking Zeus with my shoulder. I couldn't believe I was talking this way to him without chagrin. He was, after all, the king of Olympus.

"Shh," he said, but his hand fell away from my face and he did not touch me. "Lie back down. Please. You must sleep now."

"Sleep," I said, disgusted. "For what? To have more nightmares?" I turned my face to glare at him. "To regain my stamina so you can fuck me again?"

He leaned away, his eyes darkening. Hurt. A pain stabbed in my chest to see his response. But I couldn't be sorry. My words were true. I had a right to feel this way. I had been captured, taken away from all I had ever known.

"Is it so awful for you here?"

The answer to that question was not simple. Not any longer. All that I had learned from Eros taught me about potential, and that my mortal life on Earth was but one eye-blink of an all I might encompass. My fever and subsequent sensual awakening with Zeus had expanded me both physically and mentally. And my psychic rapport and mental melding with Sable left me in absolute awe. None of it was awful. None of it. It was a gift. An adventure. With tributes I could never have imagined for myself in ordinary life.

My voice came out weary, choked. "I just feel—just feel—" I couldn't finish as the tears caught me up, bent me over.

Silently, I wept. I wondered if Sable felt it.

When Zeus put his arms around me again, I let him.

Zeus said, "It is grief, *paidi mou*. A great opponent. One of the four last enemies of our kind."

19. A Dark-feathered, Tender Gesture

I woke alone. Zeus had left me sleeping. It seemed he'd wanted me to remain undisturbed today, for his servants had never arrived to wake me and order me to the baths.

I glanced around the room; its sunlit depths were cooler today, as if the room had absorbed my latest sobbing. In my chest, my heart beat slow. My breath barely swelled in my lungs. I was wrung. Dry. Worn. There was a desert inside me. A place of solitude but little peace. Quiet but wracked with unease.

Sable was sleeping. I was truly left alone.

Fully naked—no sash, the only jewelry left on me were my rings—I got up from the soft bed and walked past the sleeping raven and to the banister of the balcony overlooking the sweeps of fairy-cloud. Without really thinking about anything, I climbed over the rail's edge, looking down on more waves of cloud and sky and nothing else.

Olympus stretched behind me. I was on its edge. I could not see the palace facade from my vantage, but I could picture it from memory, the way it had first looked to me when Sable had circled the open-roofed, thousand-roomed palace. White and glowing walls. Endless rooms with checkerboard floors and golden halls. Throngs of people in its abodes and gardens, naked or glittered in gowns. Winged, horned, skin of sculptured bronze. Drunk. Teeming with life, potency, endless exultations and euphorias. An Elysia of unabating decadence, luxury, gratification.

At this moment, anyone might have traded their life for mine. But I did not think about that.

Bracing myself against the outside of the railing, leaning forward to the clouds, I counted to three. Body relaxed, giving in, I prepared myself to fall. I took one step forward.

I let go.

Nothing happened. I did not fall. I stayed where I was. My feet were planted firmly in the air on some invisible flooring I could not detect. I was still aloft. At the same height as the balcony. Trapped.

My heart beat wildly now.

Letting out a small moan, I climbed back over the edge of the railing, eyes closed now, sobs curling up into my throat again, and stumbled into silken and downy raven feathers.

My eyelids snapped open. Black softness surrounded me.

"Sable?" I started to pull back, but an edge of his wing caught me. I wanted to push into it. I did. Grasping for him. My arms going around his smooth, ruffled exterior.

For a long time, he held me very still, only the wind in its summer zephyr plushness curving delicately about us. No sound. No motion. No demand.

His magnificent fresh-feather scent of freedom surrounded me.

After a long while, he pushed me back, then forward, then steered me toward the bed with one dark wing.

"Sable," I said. My voice did not shake. I was steadier now, but still fighting the starkness inside me. "There is no way back, and no way out of this, is there?"

He pushed gently on my naked back. I fell, but by then we were at the bed, and it caught me with its pillows and cushions, my fall a soft landing at last.

He never answered my question, but stayed beside the bed watching over me, his diamond ebony eyes, his true and straight beak, his beautiful form filling my vision.

"Sable," I said. Over and over. Loving the sound of his name on my tongue.

A slow darkness pulled me in. Emotionally exhausted from my ordeal, I succumbed to new and gentler sleep, but not before I felt what I thought was a single feather dusting across my brow.

20. The Four Enemies

"He mentioned the four enemies of immortality, eh?" Eros asked, leaning back on the pillows and sunning his half naked torso. He wore only a long, black sarong today. His wings splayed free behind him, white and billowy. His bronze chest gleamed.

"Yes," I replied. "Who are these enemies?"

"Not who. What."

I raised my eyebrows at him. Out the corner of my eye I watched Sable where he stood in his usual spot surrounded by flower pots and ivy, shaded by the orange tree.

"All right. *What* are they?"

"Grief."

"Zeus mentioned that," I said. "I'm familiar with it."

"And boredom," Eros continued. "And clarity."

"Clarity? I would think that would be an asset." I fiddled with the knucklebone jacks lying on the table top.

"The moment you think you know everything and are clear on the matter is the moment of danger. For you have stopped learning, stopped observing, stopping searching."

"And the last?" I asked.

"Power."

The word settled over me like a winter storm.

It had been two night cycles since I had tried to jump off the balcony of Zeus's bedchamber. For all that time, Zeus had left me alone. My only company was Sable, and he never left the bedside, even when I got up to wander about the room, his midnight eyes following my form everywhere I went.

He never spoke to me. I read aloud to him at times. I slept. I drank a little of the wine. And I kept to myself. Even Zeus's servants never disturbed me. I had no will anyway to make it even as far as the baths.

Two days I'd stayed in that room. In that time, Zeus did not return. I felt good about that because I did not want to see him. But I confess I also felt abandoned. There was no pleasing me.

When I finally got myself to the baths and back to the throne room, tension was high on the air among the crowds, between Zeus and Eros, and with whatever Zeus was doing on his various windows. Because I was young, because I felt to be the center of Zeus's attentions, I arrogantly thought the tension was because of me.

"Power is an enemy?" I echoed Eros's last word. "You mean power like for a king, power, that friend, lover and soul of Zeus?"

"Perhaps."

"Is it not strength against enemies?"

"It can be. It can also be a burden; it can make one fickle, volatile, and temperamental. We all fight all these four enemies off and on. It is a never-ending battle with in-between moments of great purity and knowledge. They are fleeting and temporary moments. We all fight to get back to that at every turn, in every era."

Sometimes I liked listening to Eros talk. It relaxed me. Reminded me of my sky-gazing days when I lay in the fields of home and thought of the parchments I'd read that week. I could never forget that Eros was older than I might ever comprehend. With a wisdom of ages he seemed willing to share.

In that regard, with knowledge, Zeus neglected me. But in other ways, he opened me, gave me expansion to other realms in an ecstasy not unlike being one with everything. It was as if I had two halves of a whole teacher in each of them, Eros and Zeus. One for the mind. One for the body.

But today I was nervous, uptight. I didn't want to hear Eros. I was angry that Zeus seemed negligent of me, impatient. Perhaps even disappointed in me. But I had a right to my grief and therefore my moods. I clung to grief as if it were a last effort to hold onto myself.

My skin chilled as a breeze came over the balcony ruffling Sable's feathers. Little bumps rose on my skin.

Sable rarely moved except to walk behind me, head always facing straight forward. But now his head cocked. His left wing tilted down.

Eros sat up straighter, frowning.

It seemed I was the last to realize the chill was abnormal. "Something's different," I said. "I've never been cold for one moment of my time here."

"A storm is coming." Eros spoke those words almost in the form of a question.

"Storms come here?" I asked. "But there are no rooftops."

"No. Storms don't come here. That's the problem." Eros stood, his black sarong billowing behind him. He moved toward the entryway, motioning to me with one hand. "Ganymede. Sable. Inside. Now."

Quickly, I rose. Sable closed in behind me and I longed to turn and throw my arms around him and bury my face in his lushness. His safety. But I walked on, following Eros to the throne where Zeus was madly raving at one of his windows. I'd never seen him like this.

Most of the throne room was empty, which was odd. Those who remained had their own windows they were looking through, or they were busily talking with each other.

A tingle resonated on the air, like that which precedes thunder. A wind. A dampness. A darkening of the light. But when I looked up through the open ceiling I still saw only blue sky.

I moved to the throne, which was my habit. Zeus always allowed me to sit there on the padded pillows and lean against the soft-draped back. He let me bring my books, and served me endless chalices of wine.

I watched as Sable took up his place beside me, closer than usual, almost touching the arm of the throne. Eros went straight to Zeus and they began to speak rapidly in a language I could not understand.

From the oddness of the scene, I might have felt I was in danger. But I did not. Sable would protect me. I had no doubt. And Zeus's power, even if it was an enemy, according to Eros, filled any room he happened to inhabit. It gave off an aura of security.

Besides, what did immortals actually have to be afraid of? Not death, that was obvious.

"What's happening?" I asked. But no one answered me. Zeus and Eros were too intent on each other. Sable, as always, remained mute.

I watched for awhile as Eros and Zeus leaned toward a table where several windows lay. There was also a larger window open in the air before them that showed moving markers and runes that meant nothing to me.

I wasn't afraid. What harm might come to any of us? This was a mere inconvenience. Something to be annoyed at, that was all.

I ran my hands up and down the arms of the throne, feeling the smoothness of the marble. Something bumped against my hand and I looked down. In a recessed slot, a hand-window protruded. I touched its cold, hard edge with my fingertip. I did not know if Sable was watching me but I didn't care. I pulled the window from its hidden holder. By the intricate, curving marks on its sides, I could tell it was one of Zeus's.

For a moment, I stared at the clear, blank crystal. I didn't want to speak to it for fear of drawing attention. My finger found a small recessed area that Eros had taught me some time ago was a manual switch. It reacted to the heat of my skin. I held my finger on it and the picture beyond the window finally flickered blue, then green, then gold. I ran my fingertip over the smooth, cool surface, tapping against the runes that Eros had shown me, bringing the window's worlds to life.

It was easy to find Earth, but more difficult to locate the actual area on Earth I wanted to see.

I understood from Eros that Earth was not flat. I'd been raised to believe it, but had never seen the edge. I had wondered in my ponderings if, simply, land and sea joined and re-joined forever. Still, it was disconcerting to see it like a marbled ball from high, high up in Zeus's skies (the galaxy).

My fingers played on the pane of the window. No one noticed. It was not odd for me to hold such objects for reading so no one interrupted me. Zeus was distracted. Sable either didn't see, or didn't care. Or maybe he was finally on my side.

A sudden breeze blew through the throne room, bringing with it torn petals and leaves. Often, small drafts came through, but they were warm and refreshing. This wind rammed angrily about, overturning some vases of flower bouquets on a few low tables. And it was cold. I hunched closer into myself, knees drawn up, window on my naked thighs.

Zeus said something loudly in his language that sounded like a curse.

Eros responded in a rapid discourse.

I could have used the window to translate what they were saying, but I fell right into my Earth-search, barely remembering to breathe.

All around the image of the Earth-ball, sudden pictures filled up the screen, all scenes from that place. My world. Human mortals. Mini-windows within windows. People of all varieties were tilling fields, carrying water, playing in the dusty streets of cities, children and old folk, dark and light. The images whirled in my head. So many places! So many people in all types of lands, deserts, forests, mountaintops, beaches. I needed to find Tros so I looked for the rune that defined it. Too many. I could have said the word aloud but would have drawn attention to myself.

I looked alphabetically for Tros. The Earth places were all mixed up. I finally found something that sounded similar: Troy. I casually ran my finger over the rune character and the window produced new little windows of scenes. I leaned forward as I saw the city's brick wall. I saw my father's castle, grayish-blue and beautiful against a fire-opal western sky.

Through trial and error, I navigated that window to bring more images from within more windows that overlapped existing ones.

Olympus's throne room grew colder, but I ignored it.

I arrowed in on the castle. I saw the courtyard where I played with my brothers when I was very small. I saw the royal baths that connected to the castle. A kitchen garden bloomed in yellows and reds. What season was it? Spring? Early summer? How long had I been gone?

Some people were strolling through the gardens but I could not see them closely to ascertain if I knew them.

I kept touching the screen to try to see inside the castle. Finally, some pictures came, the great hall, two smaller banquet rooms and my father's throne room.

Guards stood in the great hall. The banquet rooms were empty, antique light streaming through high windows, the sconces unlit. In the throne room, I saw a crowd. I saw an old man on the throne. I widened the picture. My father sat on the throne, hair white, face cragged, back stooped. In front of the crowd stood a figure decked in shining bronze armor. I noted the dark hair, braided. A warrior, arm raised. The window gave me no sound. I hadn't mastered that control, or it was turned off.

I tried to bring the window around. Look at the crowd. I thought I saw Pal but he looked so different. And Mikkos, but he was heavily bearded so I could not be sure.

The visage of my father kept repeating on my mind, disturbing in his sudden oldness. When I finally got the window to face the warrior I saw a female, beautifully featured. The jaw-line, nose, eyes could not be mistaken. It

146

was Cinth. But she had to be at least thirty years now. She looked strong, confident, healthy.

My eyes stung to see her. But so old—all of them. How?

Just then I heard a sound like more wind, looked up and saw the open roof of the Olympus throne room turn solid and white, giving the room a curved ceiling with gold specks of stars and horns of moons painted on them. The balcony doors shut by themselves with gentle clinks. For an eye-blink, everything darkened, and then light suffused the room, as if from a hidden source. But when I looked out the sheer balcony doors, everything was dark. I should have been able to see through them, but I couldn't.

At that moment, the entirety of Olympus shuddered. I dropped the window and it landed with a loud clatter on the checkered, marble floor and cracked slant-wise across the middle.

Zeus and Eros looked up from their work, saw the broken window and looked at my stricken face. Zeus said something quick to Eros, made some motions on the air popping up more windows all around me, and came to the throne.

"Ganymede, you will have to move."

I stood, arms wrapped tightly about my body. "I'm sorry. I'm sorry."

Zeus frowned. Eros came up alongside the big chair. "Whatever for?"

I looked down at the broken window.

"I don't have time for this. Sable, escort him back to my chamber."

"No!" I backed up. "I want to stay. What's happening?"

Eros came toward me. "Ganymede, it's best to ride this out in the bedchamber."

I backed more. "Tell me what's happening. I felt this great place shudder."

"It's moving, that's all," Eros said calmly.

"Moving? Are we all doomed?"

Zeus was making a lot of quick gestures at windows that surrounded the throne now. He glanced up once at me. "Doomed? No. We are immortal. But this area is no longer stable. Someone sent a continuum wave. So we have to move or lose this beautiful abode."

I did not understand much of what he said, but it sounded dangerous. Even if we couldn't die, we might be lost. I knew the feeling well. To be displaced. I'd only just found my footing and to lose it would be unbearable.

"I broke your window."

Eros steered me to a couch. "If you won't go to the bedchamber, then sit here and be quiet. We'll talk about what you saw on that window later."

I shut my eyes hard, trying to block out the images of my family and the years gone by. It couldn't have been more than a single season that I'd been here. I opened my eyes and nodded at Eros. I noticed that Sable had come to the couch to stand at my side. Nothing ruffled him. He was always serene, unmovable.

Eros went back to Zeus and they began conversing again in their strange language. I felt another quaver from the floor and up through the couch.

"Sable," I said, "does Olympus fly?"

Yes, came the answer to my mind.

I was so surprised to receive a response I reached out to him and touched him on the edge of his furled wing. When I did, my mind was flooded with images. A green fall of water in a shaded glade. A black swan swimming. A saffron and scarlet sky. A candle in a window. A scattering of black birds across a white expanse. Stars all around me so bright I blinked back tears. Scene after scene of brilliant dusks with two or three suns setting in a line. Skies filled with moons and strange ships that looked like cities with towers jutting from the tops. An endless line of giant statues that looked like owls but weren't, all balanced on a shoreline cliff overlooking a green sea. More images flashed at me faster than I could perceive.

"Slow down. Slow down!" I said aloud.

From across the room, Eros said, "You should not be able to feel the speed at all." He thought I was referring to Olympus.

The images stopped. I replied, "I do not."

Eros said something to Zeus I could not understand, then to me, "Then who are you talking to?"

I shook my head. Even if it didn't matter to them, Sable was my secret for now. I said, "It's the wine. It spins my head."

I looked around and saw that all the guests were gone. I wondered where they went. To their rooms? Were they allowed to escape Olympus, unlike me, and go home?

I heard a torrent of words from Zeus. Even in another language, I could understand curses.

That was just before the checkerboard floor cracked open at the foot of the couch I sat on, an instant chasm the width of a grown adult roiling with darkness and stars.

I heard shouts, frantic. Before I could even get a breath to scream, a darkness encased me, soft and nurturing. Suddenly, everything went black and I disappeared.

21. Silver Dreams

I heard a voice say, "You can't kill an immortal, but the properties of its domain may be destroyed. From the fires of an unnamed star. From the deadly witch-nets that soar along the outer fringes. Or from the lappings of time that harness the power of the beginning. Nothing is more powerful than the beginning."

I swam in a sea of warm, black wine.

More voices: "There is a fifth enemy." "Boredom?" "Not that one." "Stagnation." "Yes, that one." "To live forever is to undo death, to be as legends speak of, undead." "You are a somber guest." "You must see the Dream from beyond the lucidity of the Dream itself." "The five enemies are the comfort zones intrinsic to the mindsets of your ancestors and are cancers on your Dream." "Take the elixir." "Drink and know."

The voices were echoing, unfamiliar. After awhile, I began to hear the voices of my family.

Mikkos: "He will be honored as a great king."

Pal: "In the name of Ganymede..."

Cinth's voice: "I bring gifts and peace from the East. I did it in the name of the great Ganymede who was borne up to the immortal stars and made one of them."

For a time it seemed I was liquid, dripping into myself. Rocked in the arms of a tiny, enclosed boat buried at sea. A sea of stars.

I opened my eyes and I found myself in a tiny cabin, orange fire licking a deep hearth made of colored stones, darkness all along the edges of my vision, a coiled, rough rug against my knees. I was naked, and someone I could not see covered my shoulders with a soft blanket, coming around me and wrapping it close. When I saw his face I knew him. He was the man I'd seen in my dream. The black swan. The figure bathing in a lush lagoon. Sable.

He was dressed all in black, ruffled shirt, narrow pants that hugged him all the way to his knee-high boots that shimmered in the reflected dusks of the hearth fire. His glossy black hair feathered against his ears and the collar of his shirt.

"Little human," he said. "Trailing the scattered stardust of all you have left behind. Little comet."

"Sable."

"Yes. I have you. For now."

I tried to see my surroundings. The cabin had two windows, dark, and a closed wooden door with a bar across it.

Outside it sounded as if a blizzard hunted. I had never been in a blizzard, but I could imagine it would sound like that, howling like the wildest, hunting beast.

"Are you really here with me?" I asked.

"I am all around you."

"Sable, where are we?"

"Safe," was all he said. Then he went to the fire where a pot hung over the flames and took two bowls and ladled stew into them. He placed a spoon in each and handed one to me.

"Sustenance," he said.

"We don't need that anymore."

"Food of the gods."

"Like Zeus's wine?"

"The same properties. They make you stronger for the numberless ages everlasting. Do not forget this. After millennia, you may subsist without any external energetic assimilation. You may now, but only weakness will prevail. But," and now he smiled, "it tastes good."

I put a spoonful of the stew into my mouth and flavor burst through me. My entire body began to crave the nourishment as if from instinct rather than hunger.

"Succulent?" he asked.

I nodded. "Very."

"The excellence of mind's nirvana."

Sable spoke strangely, yet from him it did not seem awkward, but more graceful than I or others I knew spoke. "Is this real?"

"Real? In what manner is anything real?"

I took a deep breath and ate, not wanting to spoil the serenity by more questions.

"Perception," Sable said, ringing his spoon against his plate. His pink lips moved gently, as if to caress his words. I was mesmerized. Every aspect of him seemed formed from natural fluidity. Elegance. "Perception. Reality blooms underneath its skies. Change the sky, the color, the scent, and perception judges. Take away judgment. Perception is free to roam. Reality unknots, is helpless before all possibility. No good, no evil. Just the palette. The paint. The alphabets. The page. The tools to create."

I remembered my lessons from Eros. "You are creating this in my mind," I said. "But it feels solid." I tasted more of the stew.

"We. Together. Your mind supplies as well as mine. And Will. Will is the final spark."

"But where are we?"

"Here. And we can have life here for as long as we like."

"But what is outside?"

"Ah, the quintessential question of all beings from every epoch. Consciousness reaching awareness must always ask this painful, wondrous query." He smiled, his head tilted back, eyes dark and scintillating. "Is this all there is?"

"But the stars?"

He rose and offered me his hand. I took it, putting my bowl aside, and went with him as he led me to one of the windows, paned in four sections. Looking out I saw them. Vast whirls of spiraling suns, some in conglomerates of cyclones that looked close enough to touch.

"Am I hearing wind?"

Sable shook his head. "You are hearing my stardrive."

"But what about Olympus?"

"Olympus always exists."

"And Zeus and Eros?" Suddenly, I felt a sharp pain in my chest. Were they all only a dream within a dream, my trip with Sable still on-going, my story starting over and over in sleep and nightmare and never waking?

"On a limping ship called Olympus. Still. They are eternal. We always find each other."

"And Tros? Cinth and Pal, Mikkos and Thon?"

"Only an alphabet away."

"What does that mean?" I put my hand to the window of stars. It was cold.

"Their paintings lie in the eternal hall of all that was and ever will be. Elusive but touching all shores of perception. Just as Ganymede runs through the fields to find his anima, his ardor, his psyche. You are that boy who runs forever and never stops, through the briskly leaping wind. The empty dusk. The full circle of a meadow. The poetry in a little book. These are your building blocks. The counterpane is village, stone, grass, traveler, and in your goldenness, your dancing autumn garden, the reign of Ganymede knows no bounds."

"But…I am just a prince of a very small country. Why?"

"Your essence is a beacon."

"Everyone's essence is a beacon."

"Yes, but you were honed by birth and fate and luck for this, for now, for us."

But I was tired of talk like this. I had never been asked. Never had the chance to choose. I spoke my thoughts aloud. "I was never given any choice."

"You were taken and set before the endless choice. You cannot yet see it."

"If I have endless choice, I can request to see my sister, my brothers? I could go home if I wanted?"

Sable took my hand in his. Before the hearth, warm and merry, hunched a couch of blue and purple shadow. He beckoned me to sit beside him. The couch had properties like Sable himself, plush, encompassing, slightly rain-scented. Sable raised his long hands and drew an invisible square in the air before us. A window appeared. Within the window I saw Tros, my father's castle, the azure Grecian skies. My heart trembled. My breath shook. I pressed my lips tightly together and watched. The picture moved through time as if unnaturally. I saw clouds rush, flowers bloom and wilt. It stopped on people at various stages, my family whom I loved, slowing down enough for me to see that Cinth wore the armor of a great warrior, and Pal never married, growing into his graying years with his lover Zeno at his side. Mikkos had nine children, each more lovely than the last, and sat the throne after my father died. I saw, as if cut into the frame, Thon die young in battle, a sword through the chest. And my mother withered soon after my father went to the grave. Tears dotted my cheeks. There were many feasts and much happiness, too, which the window showed me clearly, but finally I looked away.

"Stop. I can bear no more."

"Grief is only the beginning. The first enemy." Sable reached out and made a swift motion. The portal before us closed and only the fire in front of us remained, throwing gold-brown shadows over the walls of the hearth and on the little cabin walls.

Afterward, Sable showed me to a tiny alcove off the main room where a lush and pillowed bed of white sheets and blankets waited. I let the darker blanket fall from my shoulders and climbed in naked.

My sleep was the most serene experience I'd ever known, a pale and endless rest I never wanted to leave.

When I awoke, I lay quietly and stared at the wood-beamed ceiling, listening to the lamenting wind, or stardrive, or whatever force it was that seemed to storm the stars just outside the cabin walls, walls that seemed too thin to hold up to such a savage universe. I thought again of going to the barred door, opening it to see what would happen. But I just lay in the shadowed room, which was little more than a foyer off the main room that held the couch and the fire and the stewpot.

I wondered where Zeus had gone. And Eros. If Olympus, also, was now flying through the stars. It was strange that I thought of them just now, on waking, before any thought of my family. But Sable had shown me enough last night to leave me with fewer questions about my parents and siblings.

I sat up slowly, the softness of the sheets a caress. A voice from just beyond my vision said, "Would you like a bath?"

The question made me laugh. "Sable, if you or I or we can create any place or reality we want to inhabit, we shouldn't actually *need* baths."

"Like an infant, you do not have that control yet. You would not expect an infant to write a play, would you?" Sable walked into view, standing at the threshold to the little room.

"Of course not."

"And I did not ask if you needed one. Baths are a pleasure. Like play."

My mind instantly supplied the image of Sable, in his current human-form, bathing in the blue-green grotto of dripping fronds and ferns. A manifestation I had seen in a dream.

"Yes, I would like a bath. Is there a place to bathe in such a tiny cabin?"

Sable reached out and took my hand. For a moment, I saw a ghostly mirage of black feathers instead of fingers. My throat tightened at his foreign-ness, his beauty. I stood naked before him, holding his hand, and I was breathless.

"Come," he said, his voice like an embrace.

I followed him into the cabin's main room where the fire glowed, cinder and oak-scented, its essence surrounding my body in its warm gleam. Sable led me to a door I had not noticed before, thin wood with a greenish hue, and a round gold knob. When he opened it a rush of fragrance and sound and color assaulted my senses. Water falling, plants pollinating, a breeze holding the fragrances of grass and dew and dawn.

"This is the grotto!" I exclaimed, looking up at him. "And the lagoon. I saw it in a dream."

We entered the scene hand in hand.

"All this is in the cabin? Or—" I turned around and saw the door, which looked as if it stood house-less now, balanced on the grassy ground, a misplaced object in the wilderness.

"All is," replied Sable cryptically.

Blades of grass like silk under my bare feet. Wind like whispers. Trees bending and nodding like great beings with their own, silent agendas. The water like a melted blue jewel. I knelt at a sloping, rock outcropping and dipped my hands in the liquid. It was warm.

Without looking back, I waded into the water until I was submerged to my waist. Then I bent my knees and pushed off from the bottom, surging forward, swimming. I let out a laugh of delight.

I turned to see Sable peeling off his skin-tight black clothing and boots. His body's outward beauty was defined by long lines, lean muscles, and a swan's grace. But there was in inner candescence to him as well, a black fire that licked all around him without burning, without wilting, but giving, inspiring. I saw leaves turn and flowers nod up as if looking as he approached the pond.

He waded in and floated through the water toward me, waves rippling over his shoulders and dampening the ends of his hair.

"Ganymede, do you love to swim?"

"Yes. I learned in the deeper pools of the baths when I was six."

"This is only a modicum of how I feel when I fly through void."

Everything around us burst into color, pinks and lavenders blending with greens and golds. We floated for awhile, then swam together in circles. Faster and faster. It was like our dance in Zeus's chamber only slower, and water splashed everywhere in shawls of blue until we were laughing. Sable laughing. I had never witnessed that before.

I wondered how he was doing all this, holding reality together. It seemed effortless for him.

He left the pool first. Naturally, I followed, in a fever of pleasure at just being with him. I could not help but be attracted physically, and my eyes stared at the curves of his back and buttocks. But it was so much more than that. Eros had called it imprinting. I had imprinted on Sable. But was it the same for him? Though he had called me a beacon, taken me, I wasn't sure of his entire reasoning. Even though young, I was still a man. Yet there was enough of the boy in me to wish for a childish bliss of love without consequences or conditions. That Sable might want me as more than the beacon I was, though we had so little in common.

Such thoughts you think. His voice came into my mind.

I jerked my head up. He turned and looked over his shoulder, smirking at me.

The door, propped on nothing but grass, opened like a normal door. Sable had gathered his clothing and we walked back into the cabin. It had always been there. I simply could not see it.

22. A Difference of Souls

Upon entering the cabin, Sable did not replace his clothing, much to my personal pleasure, and I got to look at him at my leisure throughout the day.

He cooked more stew and served it with wine even more delicious than that served in Olympus.

We ate before the fire again where he opened a magic window on the air and showed me some music played by groups of people, a sound that had me nearly swooning. Beside me, his knee was bent. His thigh was long and corded. Hairless. I wanted badly to touch him.

If he could read my mind, he already knew this.

We ate more delicious stew while stars—or the stardrive—stormed about us. The bathing glade remained off to the left of my mind. I kept looking at the barred front door, wondering what would happen if I opened it and went for a walk in those stars out there. Or maybe it opened on another shaded lagoon or another world altogether.

We talked of every subject, all things I could think to ask. Eros and Zeus were on my mind a lot. The wine kept flowing in glasses shaped like flowers set before us on a crystal table.

"Zeus took me," I said. "Will he be angry that you've taken me from his sight?"

"The question presupposes much," he replied.

I was used to his vagueness and the sometimes awkward wording of his sentences.

"But I was his," I explained.

"Would I be angry if he took you from my sight? That should be your question. Or, perhaps, if he took me from your sight?"

I frowned.

"I repeat," he said. "You suppose much."

"You are loyal to Zeus, are you not?" I asked.

"We are loyal, yes, to each other. When it suits us."

"When it suits you? That is not what I have learned of loyalty."

"Mortals have different perceptions of things like that, of course. He told you he gave me my aerie. My abode away from Olympus. That is both true and false. We are friends. Cohorts on quests. A strange affinity rests between us. He thinks he saved me. This is his story. Mine is another."

"Which is the truth?"

"Exactly."

My brow furrowed in confusion. I changed tactics. "But you don't talk to him. Or appear to him like you are with me now."

"I have open connections when I wish. To Zeus. Or others. When I wish," he repeated. "I wish not, now. I do not know where Olympus is right now. And to answer your question, I do not know if he is angry." He smiled. "Are you angry?"

"You are my kidnapper as much as he. Is that what you're saying?"

"You are a beacon," was his reply. "If not us, others would have come."

I wasn't sure how to feel about that. He had ripped me from my family and home just as surely as Zeus had. That was what he had just said. Like Zeus, he should have been my enemy, both of them hated by me. Yet I felt inexorably drawn to each for different reasons. But with Sable it was more. I was attracted on so many levels to Sable, more so than ever with Zeus. Zeus had seduced me, but Sable... Sable was who I wanted to seduce. And he seemed to know that.

I asked more questions. "How many of you immortals are there?"

"No one knows. But your presence now adds one to that total."

"Is Tianzun an immortal? Why do he and Zeus fight?"

"Yes, the Jade Emperor is immortal. No one knows the exact reason why he and Zeus fight, unless it involves the second enemy of immortality: boredom."

Sable spoke of soul differences. Some souls were esoteric, some limited, he said. Some bloomed bright with fire. Others drew more inward to a diamond sheen.

"Zeus," he said, "projects from the bottom of his being." Sable clasped his stomach, pressing to indicate the energy of the umbilicus. "Proud and beautiful, assimilated from facts and things, essence of form, control, power. Origins."

He put palm to heart. "Eros comes from here. Absorbent, thoughtful, passionate. Philosophical and depthless in his observances. Considerate and loyal. Connected to the fires of comfort, hearth and wise release. Many love stories begin and end on the premise of him and him alone. For he can be romantic and experiential at the same time. His alluring force makes for risk-taking and boundless reward. He is why the rose blooms. Also, he claims to be a primordial god."

"What's that? A primordial god?"

"One of the first, of course."

I loved listening to him talk. Eros had spoken to me with quite thoughtfulness, too, but Sable had the poetic nuance and strangeness that made me want to smile. He took away all my bad thoughts. My grief, though still present, slowly became a diluted afterthought.

With Sable, I could finally relax. The muscles I had held tense for so long released. He had seen me lose my virginity and make love with Zeus. He had danced with me in spirit, spoken in my mind, read my thoughts, held me in his bodily shifting form as we traveled through the stars. He had watched me try to jump from the heights of Olympus to my fate. Of course, he had known I would not die, could not die, but he had seen me at my most vulnerable, in states of tears, suicide, ecstasy.

It seemed we talked forever. I did not remember falling asleep.

I woke in the white, soft bed again, staring at the simple wood-beamed ceiling and thinking for the first time since being taken that maybe I was lucky. Maybe, just maybe, I was the luckiest boy ever.

Sable smiled at me from the entryway. "Swim?" he asked.

I jumped up to join him.

23. *The Dance*

Here in the cabin in the stars, as in Olympus, time was strange. I slept when I felt like it, bathed, ate if I wanted, read, looked at window-games. Sable read, too, or sometimes disappeared for long periods. But I wasn't scared. I knew he'd return.

For days, it seemed, we circled each other. Smiling. Wanting. I walked about half-aroused all the time. But Sable made no moves and neither did I. I think it was because we knew we had time. And we liked the dance, both the one we had done in the air in spirit, and the one we were doing now, skirting the edges of each other, learning about more than just what we were, but who we were.

We talked often, and a lot.

Once he said to me, "The fifth enemy: Stagnation. Immortals don't have to worry about running out of energy. We just have to learn to re-master it."

He listened intently whenever I talked of Cinth, or the books I read, or how I realized, finally, that perhaps I did remember that all along in my life in Tros, lying in the fields and gazing up toward forever, I had felt different from my friends and family, and had known this ever since I could walk and talk.

"I still don't understand why I was a beacon. Zeus kept talking about my—my, uh, beauty. Which feels ridiculous. I have always hated the idea that just because of beauty a person might get a reward."

"Your beauty is Zeus's weak point, to be sure, but understand," Sable said. "It is what you exude. It is also a fact that, as I heard Eros explain to you one day on the balcony, your DNA is extremely rare and unique, made for multiple eras. Should your appearance have been other than Zeus's current esthetic for exotic beauty, or you had been born with an unfortunate disease, the beacon of you would not be affected. It would still shine. I shift and it is a pleasing gift. But by your standards, I was never beautiful."

"Am I a beacon because my mother had nymph blood?"

"Not necessarily. It can be simply a mutation of evolution. As we all are here by mere chance."

We were quiet for a time. Then I said, "My sign is the swan. You appeared to me that way in a dream once."

He lowered his eyelashes as if shy. I looked at the fire, at the colored stones embedded in the walls of the hearth, and leaned into the couch with one arm stretched out on a pillow. When I looked back at Sable a black swan sat next me. I barely caught myself from startling. I sat quite still, admiring the graceful sweep of the neck and back, the iridescent sheen of the midnight feathers. There was a sense of wildness about him that Sable had imbued in the creature, as if he had not simply taken its form but captured its essence as well.

Slowly, I reached out. My fingertips touched the lower swoop of the neck and trailed over the plumage at the center of its back.

It was like touching a fierce heart, pure being, a crux of actuality for the sake of itself without agenda. Wild.

My body surged with longing. Thrill. Love.

Without warning, Sable the man returned beside me, and my palm pressed against the smooth dents of skin at his spine. I had not touched him in this way before. The closest touch we'd shared had been from Sable in his giant raven form, mysterious arms reaching out, my body pressed into the depths of his feathers. And now. Me inside his cabin-world construct. My hand on his spine.

He turned his head and looked at me. I was hard between my legs and I wanted to cross them to hide my lack of control, but he did not look there. He stared into my eyes with an almost quizzical gaze, so unlike anyone I'd ever met.

You need not hide from me. I heard the voice in my head like an emanation from my deepest inner wells.

I wanted to be worthy of him. I wanted to be more than just Prince Ganymede, pretty youth of Tros. I wanted him.

Aloud, he said, "Of course I can feel it in every piece of air around you, every molecule." He used the Greek word *somatidio* for part or particle, then the word I'd never heard before, *molecule*. This was how he taught in his subtleties and his grace, enmeshing me. "The air is thrilled with you."

I wanted to laugh at the way he spoke, not because it was funny but because it was so delightful. If the air responded to my "thrill" at his use of words, he would feel it as well.

So the air was thrilled.

What about you? I wanted to ask.

I am thrilled as well, came the reply.

Now I did laugh. And I heard him in my mind, not laughter so much as a feeling of his smile going all the way through me.

My hand still touched his back. He leaned into it and I stroked slowly, as if I still petted the swan.

He said, "I always will remember our dancing when Zeus made love to you."

"But—" I hesitated. "I wanted it to be you. Even then."

"And yet you wanted him as well. He is a powerful force impossible to resist."

I looked away. "I never thought I might want someone who bought me as if I were no more than a slave."

"Hmm." He leaned harder into my hand. "Him? Or me?"

"Both."

"The fever you suffered is part of the changes inside you. The body becomes highly sensitized. A touch of air can arouse it. Zeus cared for you and touched you. And so you were aroused."

I lowered my face into my hands. Thinking. Maybe with Zeus I had that fevered desire, that combination of the rush of the ambrosia wine waking the force of life to an extreme level. But with Sable it was more. Something sublime. Something tremendous. My skin was feverish, yes, but in a more focused way. I was aware of it, and that focus. It was Sable who filled my thoughts and sped my heart, not wine, not a reaction to displacement, shock or even murmured endearments to my beauty.

I lifted my head, eyes and mind clear. I looked into Sable's rich brown eyes and said, "Zeus woke me." I saw us flying about the room, remembered the feeling of him falling through me as our images met on the air. "You complete me."

His bright eyes glistened. "Ganymede—"

"You can call me Gan."

"Gan. Little Earth-boy. Running to his dreams."

24. The Raven Ferries the Soul

I moved my hand up Sable's back to his shoulder, the skin silken. Was it even real?

Of course it is real.

I laughed again to hear his voice deep within me. My fingers slid along his shoulder. I drew my head forward, up, closer to him.

I wanted to kiss him.

Sable's pink lips curved up. Abruptly, he stood and my hand fell away. He loomed over me, naked, mouth open now, almost grinning. "Do you even know how to kiss?" he asked.

Of course Zeus had kissed me dozens of times. Soft and yearning. Fierce and hot. And I had kissed him back. But still I had been the recipient.

Sable held out his hand to me, palm up. I put my hand on it palm down. He gripped and pulled me up from the sofa. Then he put both hands on my shoulders and just that grip nearly undid me. He said, "For me, kissing is a delicate art."

Do you know how?

My breath went sharply into my lungs. "I think I do."

"Don't think," he said. He put his face close to mine until I could feel the warmth of his breath against my cheek. One hand came up and curved against my jaw, cupping it. He said, "When you were a little boy and they taught you to sing, you sang off-key. You broke the strings of every lyre they gave you to play. Your quill made holes in the parchment.

You did not listen to your tutors. What makes you think you know how to do this?"

My face heated. "I—I—"

"It is a dance, firm or tender, fast or slow." He rocked his head to the side and his bottom lip scarcely slipped against my own. All my senses opened now, fully aware. His breath flamed against my other cheek. A faint scent of orchids. An exhale of new leaf.

I felt his nose whisper just below my eye.

He brought his other hand up and cupped the back of my neck. Now he held my head and could tilt it any way he wished. His mouth moved with the barest of pressure against my jaw line and over it, coming up until his lips rested very gently against mine. I almost could not feel them except for the heat, the breathy dampness mouth to mouth.

I lifted my own arms, hands sliding against his lean waist.

He skimmed his lips like the thinnest of winds over my mouth, upper lip above my upper lip, lower lip pressing against it. He kissed the dent there, leading up to my nose. Then he kissed each corner of my mouth, taking his time to move back and forth. The muscles that made the lips form words spoke wordlessly to me. At the end, the softest touch of his tongue probed delicately at the center of my lower lip.

He pulled away and I realized I had not taken a breath. I gasped at the air, every hair on my body lifting slightly, my skin flushed, my cock taut between us, tingling from the dampness at its apex.

Sable's eyes watched me, a light in them like stars, like the whiteness behind my eyes that was threatening to suffuse me.

Something wisped against my erection and the air hitched in my lungs when I realized it was his own, a probing soft wand.

His hands still held me, one on the back of my neck, one against my cheek. I could not look away from him. The room appeared to swirl around us. He bent until our foreheads touched. I slid my hands from his waist to his lower back, holding him tighter, lifting my chin until our lips met again in a tentative movement, a pulsing of mouth against mouth. I copied his method with variations of my own, drawing my lips down to his chin, then up and gently catching his lower lip.

I was trembling on the edge of exploding pleasure. I needed more.

Shyly, my tongue probed the entry to his mouth. I felt him smile beneath my exploration and open. The sweetness made me drunk. The lips lightly sucked, as if needing sustenance only I could give. I probed deeper.

Show me, said the voice in my head. *Show me you know how to kiss.*

I had never had any hesitation to begin with where Sable was concerned. And now I still did not. My body knew all it wanted, and everything it wanted to do. My mouth firmed around his and I prodded his tongue which met mine in the damp heat and curled around it.

The intimacy cascaded through me. I pushed my body, my cock against him, and as he pushed back, tongue entering me, I came in long, glorious bursts of energy.

When that happened—the storm soaking my belly and his, my groans invading his own mouth—the raven became ravenous. His hands broke from my head and neck and moved under my arms, over my waist, down my buttocks. His fingers gripped there, not hard but not gentle, lifting me. My legs went around his waist as if it was natural for them to do so.

He tipped me back and onto the couch, kneeling on the edge staring down at me, eyes wide, chest heaving, cock nodding.

The physique of the treasured lover should be investigated and scrutinized completely.

There he was whispering in my mind again in his funny way, but I no longer thought it awkward. It was poetry. The fragrance of him an echoing strangeness I wanted to hold tighter and tighter to me.

I wanted his body over mine, seeing me, feeling me, finding me. Lost boy.

He heard my thoughts as his lips and hands began their explorations. As he touched me, he allowed me to touch him. One hand, partially curved, drew circles on my chest. The other, fingers spread, combed my hair from my face over and over, as if memorizing the thick and waving blond-gold textures. Slowly his fingertips walked down the planes of my face, caressing against my jaw. He lowered his head and kissed first one eye, then the other. I opened my mouth for breath and he caught it, his lips crushing. My knees bent. I almost lifted off the couch as I grabbed him around the neck, pulling him more violently to me. He made a small sound, like a muffled, cut-off laugh.

There was so much. And not enough. How do I tell in words of this dazzling moment in my story which started with a romp in the asphodel fields, a naming day feast, and then being sold to a god for the price of a few storm-footed horses and some barrels of gold?

How do I say I found my soul without sounding trite or naïve?

The colors I saw in my ecstasy have no name.

The scents were those of utter rapture: candle-flame, light, burning.

The sounds made were like those of the helpless, the dying, only we were alive and strong, soaring.

His skin slid over mine, body to body, chests meeting, hips, cocks, legs entwining. Lips and mouths feeding. Hands stroking, molding.

When Sable broke the kiss it was only so he could kiss me in other places, my neck, my chest, and the buds of my sensitive nipples. They hardened to dark berries under his tongue.

He kissed my sides, licked around my belly, the dent there, laved my hips as he lifted them, crawling back on his knees between my legs.

My cock lay hard against my abdomen. He painted a wet outline around it on my skin. I had come once already, but I never lost my erection and it rose tight and stiff, seeking attention.

He licked lightly at it, the way he had started earlier on my lips with the sheerest of touches, airy, feathery. Finally he sucked the head, holding it in the strong grip of his mouth, tongue laving all around the tip until I was nothing but flame and sparkle, nothing but the memory of a boy blown away by passion's hot wind.

I would have orgasmed fast, inexperienced as I was, if I had not just come a short time ago. Fortunate, that was, for I floated in that heated bath, riding the waves of pleasure as he sucked down on me, and up, without tiring, never seeming to need to breathe.

I was encased in euphoria. But not so drunk I couldn't want him in return, his scent, his taste, his essence.

I rose up to him, pushing him back, my cock bobbing free on the air, wet and shining. Then I hunched over my bended knees and kissed him on the chest, the belly.

When I reached his hardness I noticed the perfect shape of him, the size not large like Zeus, but still slightly bigger than me, yet perfect in every way, the right length for me to fondle, to suckle all the way down.

I licked him first all up and down the shaft, the balls. He fell onto a stack of pillows, his head back, his black bangs pushed up into a dark halo.

When I sucked him into my mouth I tasted the vine and the woods and the fields of home. I tasted summer turning into autumn, sunsets over the salted, Aegean.

Sometimes there are dreams you have when you are small or big, when you least expect them, but you just know upon waking they have to be true somewhere, somehow, in lands just beyond our sight and reach. This was like that, only right in front of me, a dream come true, and I could not get enough. My hands surrounded his hips, pulling him close.

He ran his fingers through my hair again, holding me over him. I wanted him to burst down my throat. I wanted to drink of him, take, receive. And when he finally did let go it was like drinking the milk of time itself. Fiery. Honeyed. Strong.

I licked the tip of him until the pulsings stopped and he moved back over me again, spreading my legs, lifting them to his waist where I curved them about him. He crawled up to me and kissed me, the both of us still hard, pushing against each other, slipping, catching, clutching.

He tasted me again and again, on my lips, my cock, until I was pleading. He pushed fingers dampened with our already spent love into me until I was ready to take him, then slid himself inside me like a sword to a sheath.

I cried out. Arched and came. I was in love, so it was never going to last long with me in the beginning.

Sable lasted a little longer, keeping us joined, thrusting with more care and reverence than I had ever felt from another being.

We made love in the extreme sense of that term, sinking into each other in unchecked rapture, touching the edges of things we'd never felt or seen before. Flying.

When he came inside me it was exactly like that rush of him flying into me in Zeus's chamber when we danced above the bed in the roofless room under the blue and gold-lit sky. He possessed me utterly. I felt his cool, raven-dark essence filter through me, skin, veins, bone… all the way to my heart until the embrace was complete.

Everything leaked, my eyes, my cock, and my skin in its perspiring sheen.

After long hours of loving, I fell asleep and woke as Sable was carrying me to my bed.

Our bed, he said in my mind. I looked up to see the alcove off the cabin's main room was now a luxurious bedroom with a large, four-poster overflowing with pink, purple and black pillows. It had many lamps, a window, and in the center, floating on the air, a big, yellow crescent moon.

He placed me on the velvety sheets, kissing me on the forehead. "Go back to sleep, little human."

I embraced him tightly about the neck, pulling him to me when it appeared he might leave me. "Hold me."

All the dark feathers of him, the raven, the swan, the star-travel ship, the human man, cool, hot, plush, streamlined, muscled and glossy, fell alongside me and gathered me up.

"I will not leave you," he said. *At least not for a very very long time.*

And my heart found its fullness again, like I was flying into a deep, forever-sky.

25. One Epilog of Many

Years of blood heat, burning. I no longer feel the pain of grief. No longer ail from homesickness. Once in awhile I have thoughts of some day returning to Earth, but not now. Everything that is real feels unreal. Everything that is unreal is left behind.

It is always winter at our cabin, Sable's and mine, in the middle of nowhere between the stars. The constellations are snowing. However, the bath at the cabin remains forever in summer, a blooming glade with a sapphire lagoon.

Time ceases to have meaning to immortals after awhile. And to immortals in love, a century can feel like single year.

I only know that nowadays when I look at windows to Earth, I see strange large cities with moving conveyances pulled by invisible horses. Trains. Cars. Planes. Rockets. Shuttles. I have learned their names. I have learned that Earth is not as old as some worlds, nor as young as others.

I rarely look back now, though the window technology can still show me the past. But looking back means stagnation and grief, two of our five greatest enemies.

And if I have learned only one thing about immortals, it is about moving forward. Always.

*

"where the gods walk garlanded in wisteria"

--Ezra Pound, "After Ch'u Yuan"

*

Note: *If you liked this book, you may also enjoy* **Zeus: Heir to the Gods** *coming at the end of 2017. And in 2018 look for* **Eros: Father of the Gods.**

Dear Reader:

Thank you for reading my alternate myth romance.

If you enjoyed this, you might also enjoy subscribing to my newsletter. I put it out about six times a year to announce new books and upcoming projects, and I always have sales and freebies to offer readers both from myself and other authors I enjoy reading. If you subscribe at the link below, you can get a free copy of my book "Letters to an Android".

Happy Reading!

Wendy Rathbone

Contact links for Wendy:

Facebook: https://www.facebook.com/wendy.rathbone.3

Blog: http://wendyrathbone.blogspot.com/

Newsletter sign up (you get a free copy of the critically acclaimed "Letters to an Android"): https://www.instafreebie.com/free/3ErH0

About Wendy Rathbone

I love to write. I have this thing about words and how they are used to describe beauty, love, and all the things that open us up inside to our true self, our power. Words do that for me. They make me happy. The new moon smiling, the sadness of a fallen feather at dusk, predatory eyes gazing through smoke.

The reason I write romance these days is because the overwhelming power of falling in love (which has been proven to heal even cancer) is a game-changer. It makes sad people instantly happy. It makes bleak reality look sun-warmed and friendly again.

I have written in all genres: scifi, fantasy, horror, paranormal, contemporary, erotica, romance. My poetry has won awards, publishing contracts, and was recently nominated for a Pushcart. A fiction story of mine won Writers of the Future. My fantasy/horror fiction and poetry has received honorable mentions from esteemed editor Ellen Datlow in "Years Best Fantasy and Horror". I am a hybrid writer, publishing both indie (under my press name Eye Scry Designs) and with publishers, most recently with Dreamspinner Press.

I keep coming back to romance. Gay romance. Male/male romance. Maybe it was the wonderful start I got when I was very young in Star Trek slash fanfiction. Something about that stuck. The idea of two men falling in love in a society that has winced at that sort of thing for far too long (when in ancient times and other cultures it is considered normal) is alluring. The forbidden is imminently appealing and erotic to me. Many of my themes involve abduction, pleasure slavery, indentured servitude, imprisonment. It's like, with my writing, I'm constantly breaking out of some self-imposed cage and letting my wings unfurl until I can finally fly.

This is why I write. This is what makes me burn.

All my books are available on Kindle and Createspace. So if you have the urge, go take a look. See what's on the shelf.

Love to you all!

Wendy Rathbone

Turn Left at November

Poems by
Wendy Rathbone

Visit realms of diamond rain, dust-folk lands and valleys of curses and shame. Reside in the burning moonships of dream, the silt of stars, the asphyxiation of the waking day. Meet the golden android who houses your soul. Journey through tatters of stardust down roads of sorrow. Find hope in planets of candles and crazy-eyed mermen. There you will meet November in these rich and evocative poems by Wendy Rathbone.

Unmaking Autumn

Out at the excavation site
where they are taking apart autumn
leaf by fabled leaf
the searchlights try to catch us
putting the eyes back into the pumpkins
the moon back in the witch-shaped sky
We steal blood kisses
behind the naked apple orchards.

LETTERS TO AN ANDROID
Wendy Rathbone

Cobalt is a created human, vat grown and born adult, with no human rights and indentured to serve others for the duration of his life. Liyan is a young man with wanderlust in his eyes, embarking on a career that takes him to the furthest regions of space. The two become unlikely friends and create a memorable long-distance correspondence. Through Liyan, Cobalt gets to explore the universe, living vicariously through his friend's wave transmissions. A strong bond develops between them that not even the stars can put asunder.

Now you know an android who writes poetry.

This is all your fault. Did you not read my last wave telling you extracurricular activities for my kind are discouraged? Of course this is harmless and strangely enjoyable and does not necessarily require me to leave the hotel. Pel would not care if I wrote lines of equations or nonsensical juxtaposed words. As long as the act does not bring my mental state into question.

However, in history, poetry is often written by the rebels.

So we can keep this to ourselves.

Let me know about your lieutenant's test.

And to give you peace of mind, I never believed you observed me as anything other than human.

Some people are and always will be hateful bigots. Most people are simply uncomfortable in speaking to "property." And anyway, friendship, like poetry, is also discouraged.

Your friend,
Cobalt

www.eyescrypublications.com
Also on Amazon or
order from your favorite bookseller.

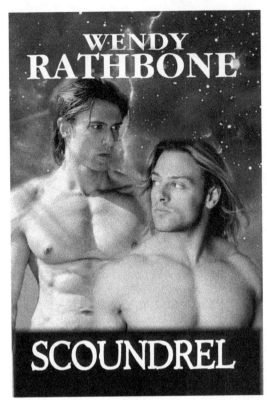

LACE
Wendy Rathbone

Lace is a being from another dimension on Earth. He cannot die and humans call his kind "vampire" and declare war on them.

Firi is a human military soldier, a trained guard, who has met Lace twice in his young life and formed a bond with him.

In a world where humans and vampires are arch enemies, where vampires are eradicated in horrible ways, where being a vampire-lover means a death sentence, can Firi and Lace ever find each other again and explore the feelings they have for each other?

Will Lace be able escape his government prison, and the amnesia that keeps him from accessing his true powers?

Can Firi, the boy he met in the woods ten years ago, ever hope to help him?

A male/male romance about secrets that can get you killed, impossible rescues, and old lovers who cannot be trusted.

www.eyescrypublications.com
Also on Amazon or
order from your favorite bookseller.

The Foundling
by Wendy Rathbone

Diego is a powerful man with a tragic past. Out on the expansive ocean in his private yacht, he discovers a beautiful and mysterious man adrift on a raft, near death. The bond that forms between them in the aftermath of Alec's rescue is one of fierce passion, though lacking in trust. Can they make it work, or will Alec's amnesia bring forth secrets so disturbing as to tear them apart? A passionately erotic love story of desire and darkness, exquisite and explicit.

I can see his struggle between gratitude and uneasiness. He is buffeted by all things new and strange. He does not know where he is from, who he is or what happened to him. He does not know me. There has not been enough time to transition between strangers and friendship.

This isolation of his is something I can identify with, but it is also a feeling no one can help him with until or unless he gets his own life back. And his memory.

If that doesn't happen, then it will take time for him to build a new life. He is polite to me, even friendly, but even a night together during a storm with his arms wrapped tight around my waist doesn't calm the surge I see inside him, the emptiness, the loss, possibly even panic. That night may have reinforced some trust in me, but so far not enough for him to completely relax.

He seeks me out, though. That's something. He sits by me at dinner when he can have any seat of his choosing. I watch him closely when he does not realize it. At dinner the following night after we had only 'slept' together, and before we go to bed again in separate rooms, I notice everything about him, how he moves, the way the air warms when he is closer to me, the dry sheen of his lips as they part for more air when he is reacting to something, or speaking, or eating.

His hands still shake. Anyone else might not notice because he keeps them clasped into fists at his sides or, while sitting, pressed tight to his lap.

I spend another fretful night alone. I dream restlessly, wild, loud and colorful visions I cannot recall at all as soon as my eyes open. All I know is the dreams leave me unfulfilled, impatient.

www.eyescrypublications.com

Also on Amazon or from your favorite bookseller.

Prince of Umberlight
Alexis Fegan Black

"If Prince of Umberlight doesn't rattle your cage, you're more dead than the undead!" -**Night Readers**

Thorn may be an 800 year old vampire, but he does not possess the ability to create others of his kind, and so he is cursed to fall in love with mortals, only to watch them grow old and die. Torn by grief, Thorn denounces his immortality and enters into a comatose oblivion for decades. When he awakens, he is no longer in London, but finds himself in a world spun into being by his own desires - a world where Time and Death do not exist, a world where it is forever autumn, where the Parish of Shadows and the River of Stars become his home. It is in this world of Umberlight that he meets Atom - an interloper into his private sanctuary, but also an impudent imp who is destined to reveal to Thorn the three dangerous elements a vampire must possess in order to become a Creator.

The Art of Brutality.
Submission to Dark Desire.
Love.

www.eyescrypublications.com
Also on Amazon or
order from your favorite bookseller.

DELLA VAN HISE

Year of the Ram

YEAR OF THE RAM
Della Van Hise

Year of the Ram was described by one reviewer as... "A spacefaring gay romance full of love, angst, and longing."

Only after Star Commander Morgan Diego becomes an exile as a result of a Galaxy Corps political blunder does he begin to realize how much he valued the companionship of his second in command - the mysterious Lucien, an Alfarian who is more elven than human, with peculiar powers & abilities which begin to unfold as he, too, realizes what he has lost.

Separated by circumstance from his former life, Morgan is thrust into a world where he must survive by his wits. When he meets a peculiar little old man calling himself Kim Le, Morgan finds himself in a situation where he is required to master The Art - not only a form of human & extraterrestrial martial arts, but a way of living and being that will alter his life forever.

At the temple, he is introduced to his new teacher, another Alfarian who begins to steal his heart - a heart which is already promised to Lucien. Torn and conflicted, Morgan struggles with the world he left behind and the world he now inhabits.

Beginning to believe he may never again return to his ship and to the friends and loved ones he left behind, he is all the more frustrated and heartbroken when a new Master arrives at the temple: a man to whom Morgan is immediately drawn both mentally and physically, a man who is strikingly familiar... yet utterly alien.

Year of the Ram is a fully-fleshed novel, approximately 97000 words, with a focus on the love story and romance angle. Set against a science fiction milieu, it explores the infinite possibilities of the human and alien heart. Sexual content is explicit, though is not the primary focus of the novel.

For those who like a romance that forces its characters to contemplate the ecstasies AND the agonies of love... you will enjoy *Year of the Ram* immensely.

www.eyescrypublications.com
Also on Amazon or
order from your favorite bookseller.

All of our titles are available directly from our website, on Amazon, or may be ordered from most booksellers. Thanks for reading us!

Eye Scry Publications
A Visionary Publishing Company
www.eyescrypublications.com

CPSIA information can be obtained
at www.ICGtesting.com
Printed in the USA
LVHW042208070722
722952LV00002B/231